Secrets Unearthed

BHOOMI

AVANISH KANDALA

INDIA • SINGAPORE • MALAYSIA

ISBN
Paperback 979-8-89544-599-0
Hardcase 979-8-89556-349-6

Contents

Acknowledgment

First and foremost, I would like to express my deepest gratitude to my family and friends for their unwavering support and encouragement throughout the writing process. Your belief in me kept me motivated and inspired.

I would also like to thank the many authors who have influenced my writing style and fueled my passion for thriller fiction, particularly James Patterson, David Baldacci, and Dan Brown. Your work has been a source of great inspiration.

Although this book is a work of fiction with no connection to real-life incidents, it was my fascination with the world of espionage and intelligence that sparked the idea for this story. My whole love and respect goes to all those agents of my country who fight for the safety of our nation.

Lastly, I want to thank everyone who has encouraged my love for reading and writing over the years. Your support has been invaluable. I apologize sincerely if anyone's sentiments are hurt while reading this book. Please forgive me with a big heart if any mistakes are found.

About the Author

Avanish Kandala is an author with a strong background in sports and a formal education in sports management. His love for reading has grown immensely over the years, fostering a deep interest in writing.

As he was growing up, he read many books by James Patterson, David Baldacci, and Dan Brown, whose writing styles had a profound impact on him. He particularly enjoyed their thriller fiction, which inspired him to write in the same genre.

The global lockdown provided him with the opportunity and time to start his writing journey. During this period, he dedicated himself to crafting his first book, pouring his thoughts and creativity onto the pages.

In his free time, he enjoys reading, playing tennis, watching movies, and working on his fitness, all of which inspire his writing. He is currently working on his upcoming books and is eager to share them with readers in the near future.

As this is his first book, he looks forward to growing and improving as a writer with each new publication and promises not to disappoint his readers. He hopes they continue to enjoy the art of reading and looks forward to sharing his stories with readers around the world.

Preface

Be prepared to dive head-first into the world of espionage and intrigue, where danger lurks around every corner and secrets lie hidden beneath the surface. In this captivating tale, the line between friend and foe is blurred, and trust is a precious commodity.

Set against the backdrop of the shadowy world of intelligence agencies, our story follows the gripping exploits of Rashid, Zoya, and operatives of the R&AW (Research and Analysis Wing), India's primary intelligence agency, as they find themselves embroiled in a dangerous game of cat and mouse, where one wrong move could mean the difference between life and death.

From the streets of Mumbai to the treacherous corridors of power, Tony, Sikandar, Rashid, and Zoya navigate a world where alliances shift like sand and trust is a rare commodity.

But as they dig deeper, they soon realize that nothing is as it seems and that their enemies are closer than they ever imagined. With danger lurking at every turn and betrayal waiting in the shadows, Rashid and Zoya must navigate a treacherous landscape where alliances are fleeting and loyalties are tested.

As the story unfolds, readers will be drawn into a world of pulse-pounding action, heart-stopping suspense, and breathtaking twists that will keep them on the edge of their seats until the very end. So, strap in and prepare to embark on a thrilling journey into the heart of darkness, where nothing is as it seems.

Chapter 1

Strong Opening

The city of Mumbai, with its undulating skyline and cramped streets, lay beneath the canopy of a moonlit night, portraying deceptive tranquility. The silver rays of the moon had cast a soothing glow upon the chaotic layer of existence as if nature itself had sought to offer respite from the tumult of urban life. Yet, beneath this veneer of calm, an undercurrent of anticipation had whispered through the air—an unspoken knowledge that the stillness was merely a precursor to a storm that was poised to break upon the world.

Mumbai was a city that defied categorization—a blend of tradition and modernity, where ancient temples stood side by side with towering skyscrapers. The vibrant life was woven with the threads of history and innovation, creating a lively mosaic that resonated with the rhythms of humanity. Its energy was infectious, a pulsating beat that echoed through the narrow alleys and bustling markets, where aromas of street food mingled with the tang of salt in the air.

Nestled deep within the fortified heart of Mumbai there, a high-tech chamber illuminated by the soft glow of countless screens buzzed with a sense of urgency. Data streams flowed like electric currents, each carrying fragments of information that were poised to coalesce into a disconcerting revelation.

At the nexus of this digital workplace stood Tony Khan, a man of unwavering determination whose gaze bore the glint of indomitable resolve. Amid the extensive assembly of monitors, each a portal to hidden domains, Tony deciphered the cryptic threats that danced across the cyber landscape. With the grace of a virtuoso, Tony's fingers danced across the keyboard, orchestrating the cacophony of data into a harmonious ensemble of insight. Emerging from the depths of the digital realm, the ominous Obsidian Dawn once again took shape—an enigmatic syndicate that had earned a reputation that sent shivers down the spines of those in the know. This shadowy organization, veiled in secrecy, wielded a unique blend of digital weaponry and clandestine networks with surgical precision. Now, their crosshairs were fixed on a critical summit: a gathering of defense ministers in Istanbul—a symbol of global unity on the precipice of disruption.

By Tony's side stood Sikandar Sher, an embodiment of silent strength whose tranquil exterior concealed a tempest of proficiencies. Whispers of his prowess as a phantom operative circulated like ghostly tales among the informed. A subtle brush of Sikandar's fingers against a concealed blade spoke volumes of his readiness for any conceivable scenario.

"Sikandar, we tread on treacherous grounds," his voice rumbled like distant thunder—a reminder that beneath the surface of apparent calmness, hidden dangers lurked. "The Obsidian Dawn has put his plan in motion, which took them months to prepare, and we now stand on the brink of unraveling their intentions."

Sikandar's gaze was unwavering as he absorbed Tony's words. "Tony, this adversary is unlike any other. Obsidian Dawn's men seek not only classified intelligence; they aim to disrupt the very fabric that binds nations together." The gravity of their mission pressed heavily upon them—what they faced was not just a matter of safeguarding lives; it was a mission to uphold the delicate balance that underpinned global stability. Tony's knuckles whitened as his grip tightened on the console, his mind racing through a labyrinth of strategies, each move a calculated countermeasure.

Screens inside the room pulsed in time with one another, recording intercepted communications and deciphering secret messages—a demonstration of the complex arrangement of the plan, whose strings were pulled by masterminds in the Obsidian Dawn organization.

Their schemes played out like a complex interplay between order and chaos, concealed under layers of cryptographic brilliance. Sikandar leaned forward, concentrating like a hawk on the hunt, meticulously dissecting the convoluted patterns with unparalleled precision.

"They're adapting," Sikandar shouted—a warning of shifting tides. "Their tactics are evolving, a response to our attempts to thwart them."

Tony's resolve was unwavering, his lips pressed into a firm line. "We cannot allow them to outpace us. The Istanbul Summit represents a beacon of hope. We must ensure that this beacon does not fade."

As the screens continued their frenetic display, a profound silence descended—a hush heavy with the weight of responsibility. They were no longer mere operatives; they were the sentinels of equilibrium, standing steadfast against the tidal wave of chaos threatening to engulf the world. Tony turned to Sikandar with a determined expression. "We need a plan—a master strategy to dismantle their network." Sikandar's eyes gleamed with predatory focus. "And we must act swiftly before their nefarious scheme comes to fruition."

The malevolent plan of the Obsidian Dawn was a ticking time bomb, the countdown to a cataclysmic event drawing closer with each passing moment. Upon the shoulders of Tony and Sikandar rested the fate of nations. Within the softly illuminated chamber, amidst the hum of screens, an unbreakable alliance was forged—not just by circumstance but by an unspoken oath of duty.

As the countdown pressed on, the approaching dawn cast elongated shadows—a tangible manifestation of the Obsidian Dawn's influence, threatening to plunge the world into darkness. Yet, undaunted by the encroaching storm, Tony and Sikandar remained resolute, poised to confront the chaos head-on, emerging from the crucible as symbols of hope and unwavering determination. Their alliance, a testament to human resilience, stood as a formidable bulwark against the impending abyss.

The relentless countdown continued, and the sky outside the chamber's fortified walls began to lighten, marking the approach of organization's evil plan. It was a harbinger of impending havoc, threatening to cast a shadow that would stretch across nations, enveloping them in a shroud of uncertainty. Nevertheless, Tony and Sikandar remained undeterred, their determination unwavering in the face of the looming storm.

With each passing moment, the city of Mumbai stirred from its slumber, its inhabitants oblivious to the war taking place inside the walls of the intelligence enclave. The metropolis was a canvas painted with a variety of colors and stories, and the streets were alive with activity. Underneath this colorful front, a fight of brains and cunning was being fought, with Tony and Sikandar leading the charge against the forces attempting to bring about global anarchy.

The buzz of the screens seemed to echo the heartbeat of a world on the brink, a symphony of data pulses that served as a reminder of the stakes at hand. Within this digital orchestra, Tony and Sikandar held their instruments—keyboards and blades—ready to play their part in the crescendo that was building to a climax. Their alliance was a testament to the unbreakable bond formed through shared purpose, a bond that transcended the boundaries of nationality and identity.

In the midst of this turmoil, a map of Istanbul illuminated one of the screens. The markers of the impending summit glowed like beacons of hope, their significance magnified by the danger that lurked in the shadows. Tony and Sikandar's task was not only to protect these markers but to ensure that the promise of unity they represented was not crushed under the weight of malevolent intentions.

As the last moments of darkness waned, the chamber seemed to pulse with a renewed energy. The silence was broken by the tapping of keys, the hushed conversations between Tony and Sikandar, each word carrying the weight of a nation's fate. They strategized, analyzed, and planned, their minds working in harmony to outsmart an adversary whose digital footprint was shrouded in darkness.

"Sikandar, we must find their weak points, exploit their vulnerabilities. This alliance of nations cannot be allowed to crumble."

Sikandar nodded in agreement, his eyes never leaving the screen as he analyzed patterns within patterns. "Indeed, Tony. To dismantle their network, we need to think like them, anticipate their moves."

As the minutes ticked away, Tony's resolve only grew stronger. "We have the advantage of surprise. The organization may have devised this plan meticulously, but they couldn't account for our tenacity and skill."

Sikandar's lips curved into a determined smile. "Let them underestimate us. In their arrogance lies their downfall."

The screens continued to pulse with data, a visual representation of the battle being waged in the realm of zeros and ones. With a shared understanding, Tony and Sikandar knew that this was not just a fight for the sake of victory—it was a fight to preserve the essence of humanity's progress and cooperation.

Tony's voice was steady, even in the face of uncertainty. "Our plan needs to be multi-pronged. Disrupt their communication, expose their operatives, and sow confusion within their ranks."

Sikandar's gaze intensified, his fingers tapping rhythmically on the console. "We'll need to infiltrate their layers without being detected. Any misstep could spell disaster."

Tony's eyes met Sikandar's, the bond between them unspoken yet profound. "We've faced formidable adversaries before. This is no different. We stand on the precipice of history, and we will not let chaos prevail." With the dawn inching closer, Sikandar's voice carried a sense of purpose. "Tony, let's make sure that when the sun rises, it brings with it the light of victory, dispelling the shadows that sinister network seeks to cast."

Tony's gaze shifted back to the screens, a fire in his eyes. "Sikandar, this is our city, our world. We will not let it fall to chaos."

As the Istanbul summit neared, the symphony of screens reached a crescendo, a culmination of months of effort and anticipation. The fate of nations hung in the balance, the outcome hinging on the choices and actions of a few determined individuals. Tony and Sikandar were no longer just operatives; they were architects of destiny, forging a path through the storm to ensure that the beacon of hope remained unextinguished.

Chapter 2

Dynamic Characters

In the heart of Mumbai, where the chaos of life played out on the streets, a secrecy resonated within the walls of a nondescript building. This was the headquarters of the Research and Analysis Wing (R&AW), a name that evoked intrigue and curiosity in equal measure. For within these walls, a network of skilled individuals worked tirelessly, dedicating their lives to the pursuit of knowledge and the protection of their nation.

The birth of the Research and Analysis Wing (R&AW) was shrouded in the shadows of a newly independent India, a nation finding its place on the global stage. It was a time of uncertainty, of shifting alliances and emerging threats, and the need for an agency that could navigate this complex landscape became apparent.

In the aftermath of independence, India's leaders recognized the critical importance of having an organization that could gather intelligence from external sources, analyze global developments, and provide insights to safeguard the nation's interests. Thus, R&AW was born, its foundations rooted in the vision of safeguarding India's sovereignty in a world fraught with challenges.

The agency's origins were modest, its early years marked by a handful of dedicated individuals who believed in the power of information. These pioneers, operating from the shadows, laid the groundwork for what would become a formidable force in the world of intelligence. They understood that in an interconnected world, knowledge was power—an axiom that would shape R&AW's ethos for decades to come. As the Cold War cast its long shadow across the globe, R&AW found itself caught in the crosscurrents of geopolitics. The agency's operatives operated discreetly, gathering intelligence from various corners of the world, deciphering coded messages, and piecing together the puzzle of international intrigue. It was a time of covert missions and high-stakes diplomacy, where every move carried the weight of national security.

The agency's mandate evolved over the years, adapting to the changing dynamics of global politics. Its operatives worked tirelessly, often operating in the shadows, to gather information on emerging threats, counteract surveillance, and safeguard India's interests. They were the unsung heroes of a nation, the silent watchers who navigated the maze of international relations with finesse and precision.

R&AW's reputation grew, its presence felt on the world stage. Yet, its operations remained veiled in secrecy, known only to a select few within the government. Trust was paramount, and each operative understood the gravity of their mission. They were the embodiment of India's watchful eye, the sentinels against threats both known and unseen.

As the years passed, R&AW's operations expanded, its capabilities diversifying to meet the challenges of a rapidly changing world.

Its operatives hailed from diverse backgrounds—technological experts, linguists, diplomats, strategists, and those with unique talents forged in the crucible of conflict. Each operative was a thread of force in R&AW's operations, contributing their skills and experiences to the greater whole. Similarly, two figures emerged as enigmas in their own right—Tony Khan and Sikandar Sher. Their paths had crossed within R&AW's hallways, drawn together by a common goal that transcended their differences.

Tony Khan was not born into a life of espionage. In actuality, his childhood had been filled with mundane activities like school, friends, and the occasional puzzle. But it was amid those innocuous difficulties that a dormant genius developed. Tony spent hours as a child battling his wits with complicated crossword puzzles, cryptic riddles, and mind-bending Sudoku.

His parents, both professors in their own right, recognized and fostered his talent. Tony had solved sophisticated codes that had baffled seasoned cryptographers by the age of fourteen. R&AW took note at that point. They saw in him a remarkable gift, a person with the uncommon capacity to detect patterns where others saw only chaos.

His recruitment into R&AW was a watershed moment. Tony's world stretched beyond the limits of his puzzle-filled chamber to the broad halls of the agency. Within those walls, he found himself surrounded by minds that matched, and occasionally exceeded, his own. He became a part of a covert society where codes were weapons and decoding were a form of diplomacy.

Tony's approach, not his abilities, distinguished him. He saw each puzzle as a reflection of the larger universe, and each solution as a step towards grasping the bigger complexities of life. He realized that intelligence was about perceiving the links that held the world together, not merely gathering information. As a result, Tony Khan became R&AW's puzzle solver, decoding transmissions that contained the key to covert operations. His fingers danced over keyboards, arranging an array of data into a work of art. He peeled away layers of secrecy with each decryption, revealing the hidden agendas that threatened global stability.

Unlike Tony's mundane childhood, Sikandar Sher's story unfolded in the midst of a struggle. He grew up amid the echoes of gunfire and the shadows of conflict, having been born in a place where warfare was a frequent companion. His parents, both humanitarian workers who had dedicated their lives to alleviating others' suffering, instilled in him a feeling of responsibility and compassion.

Sikandar faced the harshness of war at a young age—the anguish of loss, the struggle for survival. These encounters carved themselves into his very essence, molding his fate in ways he could never have predicted. As he grew older, so did his determination to stand up to oppression and defend those who couldn't defend themselves.

Sikandar's path led him to become a freelance journalist, a man who went into conflict zones equipped with a camera and a desire to tell the unheard stories. He captured the plight of those caught in the crossfire, bringing their situation to the attention of the world. His journalistic endeavors, however, were only a portion of his objective.

Sikandar's route crossed with a hidden operation planned by R&AW during one of his deployments. The agency was drawn to his unique views and understanding of conflict dynamics. They saw in him a man who could not only document but also navigate the shadows with ability and precision. Sikandar's recruitment into R&AW represented the beginning of a new chapter in his life, one in which his experiences in combat zones became assets, his senses sharpened to a razor's edge. He rose to prominence as a defender of the shadows, a deterrent to dictatorship, and a force to be reckoned with on the battlefield of surveillance.

His background had taught him the art of survival; now, his abilities were focused on averting the battles that had damaged his youth. Sikandar's attention was fixed on Tony's words, his history engraved into the creases on his face. He understood that their task was more than just saving lives; it was also about maintaining the delicate balance that sustained global security.

After a few years of recruiting Tony and Sikandar, a third figure entered the stage—Aisha Kapoor whose youth was steeped in diplomacy, a life maneuvered via the halls of power and the whispers of high society.

She grew up in a world where conversations were strategic and alliances were formed over exquisite dinners, as she was born into a family with significant roots in international relations. Despite the grandeur, Aisha always felt a tug towards something deeper—a need to make a concrete influence, to transcend the divides that separated nations.

Her interest in geopolitics began at a young age, as she watched her parents manage the rise and fall of diplomacy. She absorbed their dialogues, their intricacies, and their capacity to overcome cultural divides. Aisha became a bridge between nations inside R&AW, a diplomat who operated in the shadows. Her interactions were subtle, and her chats were rich in significance. She could gather information without raising suspicion and develop connections without making a fuss. In a world where knowledge was king, Aisha Kapoor wielded her empathy like a weapon, forging connections that crossed borders and brought different voices together.

Another member of the team was Maya Sharma, a force to be reckoned with in the domain of technology. Her passion with technology began as a child and gradually turned into an obsession. She grew up with the rise of the digital age, when screens carried the promise of limitless possibilities. Maya dug deeper, immersing herself in the realm of codes and algorithms, while her peers were content with games and social media.

Her selection into R&AW attested to her brilliance. She rose to the position of digital maestro at the agency, a woman who could navigate the virtual world with unrivalled ease. Maya was a cyber spying powerhouse, from intercepting communications to hacking encrypted databases. Her passion was only matched by her conviction that technology could be used for good.

Maya understood that in the digital age, knowledge could be used as both a weapon and a shield. She was adamant that it be utilized for good, that the darkness of the internet world be enlightened by the light of truth.

And then there was Arjun Mehta, a man whose understanding of human nature was a testament to his years in the field. He began his career as a young officer with the Intelligence Bureau, India's domestic intelligence organization. For years, he had walked a delicate line between revealing secrets and safeguarding his own. But it was a botched mission that actually defined him. Arjun found himself in a scenario where the lines between good and wrong were blurred after being sent to infiltrate a covert operation. His instincts had guided him, but the mission took an unexpected turn, leaving him with apparent and hidden scars. It was an operation that had made him rethink not only his own actions, but also the nature of the intelligence game itself.

Despite the scars, Arjun's understanding of human nature remained unrivalled. He could read people like open books, accurately determining intentions and motives. His experiences had taught him that intelligence was about comprehending the complicated mix of emotions and impulses that propelled individuals, not just data. His hiring at R&AW was a logical next step, recognizing his particular knack for unravelling the complexities of human behaviors. Arjun's views were useful, and his ability to predict adversary movements set him apart. He was a guy who had learned the hard way that even the sharpest brains might stumble, and that the line between success and failure was frequently razor thin.

They were the best R&AW had to offer in a world where shadows masked hidden agendas and secrets were whispered on the wind. They were great individuals; as a group, they were a force to be reckoned with. Their experiences had formed them into distinct facets of a complicated whole, each bringing their own set of strengths to the table of defenders. They had been refined into precision weapons in the crucible of their experiences, ready to strike at the core of threats that dared destroy the world.

Chapter 3

Ticking Countdown

Back in the R & AW's headquarters in Mumbai, a room of significant importance was full of activity. It was a room like no other, a place where the dark order of the world was dissected, and solutions were born from the fusion of intellect and experience.

The command center was dimly lit, the glow of computer monitors casting a green and blue hue on the faces of the team assembled there.

Anxiety along with high spirits hung in the air as they prepared to dismantle Obsidian Dawn, an intangible organization that had escaped capture for far too long.

The walls were covered in maps and charts, each with a maze of red lines and mysterious symbols. One wall was dominated by a big screen that displayed live data feeds from around the world. The team known as "Alpha Five" which consists of Tony Khan, Sikandar Sher, Aisha Kapoor, Maya Sharma, and Arjun Mehta had gathered here, each bringing their own set of expertise to the work at hand.

Tony Khan, the problem solver, sat poised in front of a computer, his fingers neatly sliding across the keyboard, striking the keys hard to hack into their systems. Sikandar Sher, the mysterious guardian of the shadows, stood alongside him, reading over a stack of intelligence reports.

While other three were analyzing the maps, and some additional reports that laid down of the table in center. Tony broke the silence, his voice measured and confident. "Obsidian Dawn's plan is nothing short of outrageous. They are aiming for the upcoming Istanbul summit, and their strategy is multifaceted. Transportation, communication, and security are all under attack."

Sikandar nodded in accord. "We've been following this organization for a long now. They're not your typical foes. They understand how to exploit flaws in even the most protected systems. This will not be an easy takedown."

Aisha Kapoor stood and, chimed in. "I've managed to infiltrate their communication network to some extent. They are incredibly meticulous in their planning, using coded messages and layers of encryption. Deciphering their intentions fully will take time."

Maya Sharma, the digital maestro, projected a map onto the central screen, highlighting potential weak points in Obsidian Dawn's scheme. "I've been working on tracing the movements of their operatives on the ground. We've identified several key figures, but their network is expansive. We must locate their linchpin."

The team then looked at the last member Arjun Mehta who was still figuring out something, soon he leaned against an adjacent table, his eyes fixated on the map. "Our best chance is to destabilize their leadership and cause confusion among their ranks." We can disrupt their agenda if we can cause discontent among their senior members."

The team considered the magnitude of the situation with quiet determination. Obsidian Dawn was a dangerous adversary, and the Istanbul meeting was critical to the nation's security. Tony Khan's firm and unrelenting voice boomed out once more. "There is no such thing as failure." The stakes are simply too great. It's time to put our skills to the ultimate test and finally bring Obsidian Dawn down."

The room was filled with a renewed sense of purpose as team members exchanged nods. They knew the mission ahead would be dangerous, but they were R&AW's best—a group of individuals refined into precision weapons by their experiences, ready to meet Obsidian Dawn in the shadows.

The team then decided to take a short break, as they had been in the room for a long time now.

Tony and Sikandar sat at the coffee table, while the other three spread out in the cafeteria to get a quick bite.

Sikandar told, "We need to come up with a plan to blow their covers out, they're too cunning."

Tony nodded as he sipped the coffee. The other members joined the table too, and soon they engaged in the casual conversation. Some fun banters and laughter echoed in the empty cafeteria. A much-needed break to free their minds, and come fresh as the task ahead was difficult and needed them to be at their absolute best.

They returned to the room after a short break. The time was here to devise a strategy to demolish the organization. Tony, Sikandar, Aisha, Maya, and Arjun descended into the core of Obsidian Dawn's complicated plot, laptops open and maps in front of them. Tony and Sikandar, who had been following the organization for a while, were able to provide crucial insights into their strategies. Tony reclined back in his chair, his gaze fixated on the screen, which displayed the specifics of Obsidian Dawn's studied destabilization strategy. "Their strategy is multi-pronged," he started,

"They intend to hit multiple pillars simultaneously, causing widespread chaos."

Sikandar nodded, his attention drawn to intercepted transmissions. "Transportation is a high priority." They intend to destabilize important transportation hubs, producing disruption in the movement of people and goods. It will cause chaos and disarray."

"I've managed to pinpoint some of their encrypted channels," Aisha, who had been monitoring the organization's communications, remarked. We may be able to lure them into traps if we intercept their messages and feed them false information."

Maya used the middle screen to illustrate potential flaws in Obsidian Dawn's approach. "We must concentrate on their ground forces." We've discovered a number of prominent personalities who play critical roles. If we can take them out, it will create confusion within their ranks."

Arjun leaned across the table, studying the personalities of Obsidian Dawn's key members. "It is critical to understand their motivations and weaknesses." We can use psychology to set them against one another."

The team members continued to debated their strategy. It was a delicate blend of exact timing and exploiting Obsidian Dawn's flaws. As the night progressed, preparations were made, messages were intercepted, and techniques were modified.

Obsidian Dawn had underestimated R&AW's defenders, a crew refined through their experiences. The struggle in the shadows had begun, and the destiny of the Istanbul summit was now in their skilled hands.

Tony looked at Sikandar with spark in his eyes. "Sikandar, we've been following these men for years. You're familiar with their patterns. "Can you predict their next move?"

Sikandar leaned across the table, studying the reports again. "I think I can. Precision and timing are important to Obsidian Dawn. If we mess with their time, we mess up their entire scheme. I'll work with Aisha to feed them false information and throw them off guard."

Aisha agreed with a nod. "Every tool at our disposal must be used." Misdirection could be our most valuable asset."

Maya's chipped in too as she followed the digital trails of Obsidian Dawn's agents. "I'll continue to monitor their online activities." We'll know we're on the correct track if they make any abrupt adjustments in their communication habits."

"We have our work cut out for us, but we've faced tougher challenges before," Arjun finished, his gaze never leaving the psychological profiles. We're a team, and together we'll take down Obsidian Dawn and protect the world."

The room remained busy as the clock struck twelve o'clock. The team had been working nonstop, with each member offering their knowledge to fine-tune their strategy against Obsidian Dawn. The control center's subdued lighting created a calm yet focused environment. As he decrypted another encoded message, Tony Khan's eyes swept across lines of text, fatigued but resolute. "Their communications are a complex web, but we're starting to untangle it." We must always be one step ahead."

Sikandar Sher had laid together a set of charts that traced Obsidian Dawn's movements around the world. "These guys have travelled extensively, and their operations are meticulously planned." If we mess with their time, we mess up everything."

Aisha Kapoor, who was still infiltrating communication channels, looked up. "I've left a trail of breadcrumbs for them to follow." Let's see whether they'll bite."

Maya Sharma's computer prowess was on display as she continued to watch Obsidian Dawn's operatives' activities. "Their digital footprint is extensive, but we've identified a few gaps." We may gain an advantage if we can exploit them."

Arjun Mehta, paused for a moment to think. "Keep in mind that our opponents are not only skilled; they are also deeply committed to their cause." That dedication must be used against them."

The team's resolve was unwavering, but the long hours had taken their toll. Fatigue set in, but their commitment to the objective kept them going.

Tony Khan stood up, stretching his tired muscles. "We've made progress tonight. Tomorrow, we put our plan into action."

Sikandar nodded, weariness etched into the lines on his face. "We've faced tougher challenges. This is just another battle in the shadows."

Aisha gave a tired smile. "Obsidian Dawn won't know what hit them when our misdirection takes effect."

Maya too jumped in and said, "their digital fortress won't hold up for long under our scrutiny."

Arjun's gaze shifted from the psychological profiles to his team members. "Remember why we're doing this. It's not just about dismantling an organization; it's about protecting our nation and the world."

With renewed determination, the team members dispersed, each taking a well-deserved break before the day of reckoning. The command center, a witness to their tireless efforts, fell into a momentary silence.

As the clock ticked towards dawn, the defenders of R&AW found solace in their unity and their shared purpose. Obsidian Dawn had underestimated their resolve, and in the coming hours, they would reveal the full extent of their expertise.

The midnight hour passed, leaving behind a room filled not just with maps and screens but with the collective will of individuals who had been forged into a formidable team—a team prepared to confront Obsidian Dawn, even in the darkest corners of the world.

Next day, the team *Alpha Five* gathered with the first light of day flowing through the control room's windows, their dedication unshakable and the weight of their mission heavy on their minds. They understood they were the nation's last line of defense as the approaching Istanbul conference hung in the balance. Tony Khan spoke to his squad, saying, "We've been through a lot together, and today is our ultimate test." The stability of the globe depends on our shoulders, and I believe in each of you." Sikandar Sher, the, stood by Tony, his might palpable. "Our strength comes from our unity." Whatever challenges we encounter, we tackle them together."

Aisha Kapoor joined the chorus of determination. "Obsidian Dawn is a formidable foe, but they have no idea how strong our resolve is." We are more than just a group; we are a power to be reckoned with."

Maya Sharma showed a map of the trip to Istanbul onto the central screen. "Our strategy is in place, but we must act quickly." The clock is ticking."

Arjun Mehta reminded them of their mission's ultimate purpose. "We're not just protecting a meeting; we're saving the world from chaos." Let us recall why we are doing this."

A sense of purpose filled the room as the team members prepared to leave, but their joy was fleeting. Aisha's attempts to break Obsidian Dawn's firewall ran into an unforeseen stumbling block. Obsidian Dawn's hackers had anticipated their every action, halting their progress in real time.

As she battled the inexorable security measures, Aisha's expression darkened. "This is terrible. It's as though they're one step ahead of us, reading our every move."

Tony's expression darkened as he realized the gravity of the issue. "We can't afford to waste any more time here." Our final destination was always Istanbul. We must arrive immediately." Sikandar smacked the table with his closed fists, his eyes blazed with determination, and nodded to his crew. "This makes no difference. We proceed as planned, but now we must deal with this on-the-ground issue." Maya was unfazed by the unexpected setback. "Our expertise isn't restricted to the digital realm. We keep them with us."

Arjun, understanding their disappointment, accepted the challenge ahead. "This only emphasizes the significance of our mission." In Istanbul, we will battle Obsidian Dawn head on, and we will win."

The team's initial disappointment turned into newfound determination. They would not be deterred from their purpose despite this setback. Tony's unshakeable belief inspired his comrades, who were now more driven than ever.

The weight of the world's stability lay on their shoulders as they exited the room. Obsidian Dawn had thrown a curveball, but the R&AW defenders were prepared to adapt, conquer, and confront the darkness in Istanbul. Their voyage had taken an unexpected turn, but they remained determined to keep the meeting safe at all costs.

Chapter 4

Veil of Shadows

"It's gonna be a long day, my friends, so y'all better be prepared for it."

"Firstly, we gonna have an official meeting, because we will need some additional help, as the Istanbul ground is foreign to us," Tony's voice filled the meeting room, pulling the attention of the Alpha Five team members who had gathered around the big rectangle table.

The team, Tony Khan, Sikandar Sher, Aisha Kapoor, Maya Sharma, and Arjun Mehta, sat in silence, their faces were determined hinting their hunger to dismantle the dark organization, and restore the world order.

Tony too settled into his chair, just as the team thought they were about to probe into their strategy, the room's heavy door creaked open, and another figure entered.

The newcomer was a man in his late forties, his frame sturdy and his shoulders broad. His beard bore the marks of experience, a blend of black and grey hairs. This was Vikrant Roy, a legend within the ranks of the RA&W.

Vikrant had started his journey as an undercover operative for the agency in his early twenties. His exceptional fieldwork had earned him promotions and a reputation for being one of the best in the business. Now, he served as the head of covert operations, guiding and leading agents like Alpha Five. The team members rose from their seats, their expressions were full of respect and reverence for the man who had not only been their superior but had also earned their deep admiration. Vikrant Roy was a name of excellence in the world of intelligence. "Easy, lads," Vikrant said with a nod, acknowledging their respect. He motioned for the Alpha Five team to take their seats, and they did so, their attention now fully focused on the man who held a wealth of knowledge about the upcoming mission.

Mr. Vikrant's presence in the room signaled the gravity of the situation, and the team understood that they were about to receive critical information that could make or break their mission.

"Thank you for being here, Mr. Roy," Tony began. "We understand that you've been to Istanbul, and your experience there will be invaluable to us."

Vikrant nodded, his gaze shifting from one team member to another. "Istanbul is a complex city, a crossroads of cultures and influences. It's both ancient and modern, and navigating its terrain can be challenging. But with the right guidance, you'll find your way."

As Vikrant spoke, he delved into a detailed account of Istanbul's unique landscape. He described the winding streets of the Grand Bazaar, the historic beauty of the Blue Mosque, and the bustling energy of Taksim Square. He emphasized the need for the team to blend in seamlessly with the local population, to become shadows in the midst of a rich cultural city.

"You won't be alone in this endeavor," Vikrant assured them. "The RA&W has contacts in Istanbul, informants who can provide you with crucial information and support. You'll need to establish connections and trust, as your success depends on local cooperation."

Sikandar Sher leaned forward, his eyes fixed on Vikrant. "Do we have names, contacts, or locations?"

Vikrant nodded. "Yes, we have a few names that can help get you started. You'll meet a contact known as Emir, who has deep roots in the city's underworld. He can guide you to potential allies and sources of information. But remember, trust is earned in this world, and you'll need to tread carefully."

Aisha Kapoor, always attentive to details, inquired further. "How can we recognize this, Emir? Any distinctive traits or markers?"

Vikrant offered a faint smile. "Emir is known for his silver-gray hair and a penchant for wearing dark sunglasses, even at night. He'll be your gateway to the underground network, so keep an eye out for him."

Maya Sharma, the team's digital maestro, was eager to ensure their communications were secure. "What about communication protocols? How do we stay in touch with you and the local contacts?"

Vikrant handed over a set of encrypted devices, each programmed with a secure channel. "These devices are untraceable and will allow you to maintain contact with both me and your local contacts. Use them wisely and sparingly. We don't want to draw any unnecessary attention."

Arjun Mehta, looked pensive. "What's our first move when we arrive?"

Vikrant's gaze turned serious. "Your first priority is to establish a safe base of operations. Emir will assist you in finding a secure location. Once you're settled, we'll proceed with gathering intelligence on Obsidian

Dawn's activities in Istanbul. Remember, time is of the essence."

With the details of their mission laid out and the guidance of their seasoned mentor, the Alpha Five team was ready to board on this challenging endeavor. They had a city to navigate, alliances to forge, and a dangerous adversary to confront.

While the Alpha team was leaving, Vikrant asked Tony and Sikandar to stay, as they three know each other from a long time. Vikrant was leaning against the wall, while his eyes fixed on the large screen lit by the projector.

"It's a high-stakes game we're playing, gentlemen," Vikrant remarked, his voice low.

"The mission relies on two unknown individuals named Rashid and Zoya, who are cunning adversaries, and they've managed to infiltrate the summit at the highest levels." Vikrant further added.

"But how would we spot them, nobody has ever seen them, we don't have any photograph or intel on these two" Tony questioned Vikrant.

"Well, that's what I'm also afraid of. This is why I'm telling you both alone, as you're our best bet, your job is not only to dismantle the threat but also take out these two too," answered Vikrant

Sikandar, always the pragmatist, added, "Our intel indicates that they have a well-arranged plan in motion. We need to disrupt it before it's too late." Vikrant's experienced eyes scanned the room, taking in the maps and documents scattered across the table. "Our advantage is that we know the enemy and their intentions. We've seen their playbooks before."

Tony folded his arms, a thoughtful expression on his face. "Vikrant, what do you think their endgame is? Why risk so much on this summit?"

Vikrant considered the question carefully. "Power, Tony. Rashid and Zoya, the face of Obsidian Dawn has always been driven by the pursuit of power. And what better way to gain it than by disrupting the world order on a global stage?"

Sikandar interjected, "But they must have a specific objective within the summit, something that serves their long-term goals."

Vikrant nodded. "Agreed. Our task is to uncover their specific objective and thwart it. That's where our team's skills and your leadership come into play."

Tony turned to Sikandar, a determined look in his eyes. "Sikandar, we need to infiltrate their inner circle, gain their trust. It's a risky move, but it might be the only way to get close enough to disrupt their plan."

Sikandar nodded in agreement. "I've been working on a plan for just that, Tony. We have a few leads on potential allies within their ranks. If we can turn one of them, we might have a shot at unraveling their plot."

Vikrant chimed in, "Remember, trust is a double-edged sword in this world. They'll be cautious, and any misstep could expose our true intentions." Tony took a deep breath and looked at his team. "We knew this mission wouldn't be easy, but it's what we've trained for. We have the skills, the knowledge, and the determination to stop Obsidian Dawn. Let's stay focused and execute the plan."

Sikandar's eyes glinted with resolve. "We'll use every resource at our disposal, Tony. Failure is not an option."

Vikrant pushed himself away from the wall. "Remember, gentlemen, the world is watching. Our actions today will determine the course of history. Let's make sure it's a history that favors order over chaos."

As they left the briefing room, the weight of their mission bore down on them even more heavily. But in their hearts, there was a fire of determination that burned brighter than ever. Obsidian Dawn had thrown a curveball, but they were prepared to adapt, conquer, and confront the darkness in Istanbul. The destiny of the Istanbul summit and the world's stability rested in their skilled hands, and they were ready to rise to the occasion.

While team Alpha Five was on the march, the dark clouds of terror were looming over the city of Istanbul, where the soft breeze carried the aroma of spices and the faint echoes of mosque prayer calls in the center of Istanbul, a city where antique and modern architecture coexisted. A mesmerizing combination of history and culture, Istanbul's splendor left a lasting impression on everyone who saw it.

Amidst this breathtaking backdrop, a sleek black sedan pulled to a stop along a cobblestone street, its engine roaring in the serene afternoon. As the car's doors opened, two enigmatic figures emerged, each exuding an air of power and intrigue. Rashid al Mansoor, a man of imposing stature with a chiseled jaw and piercing eyes, stepped out first. His tailored suit and confident conduct marked him as a man of influence. Beside him was Zoya Inayat, a woman of undeniable beauty and intelligence.

Her eyes held a depth of knowledge and determination that matched Rashid's.

The city's beauty seemed to pale in comparison to this pair, their presence commanding attention as they walked in tandem towards the palace.

Rashid's charismatic voice broke the silence, a prelude to their impending actions. "Zoya," he said, his words measured and filled with intent, "the time has come to set our plan in motion. Istanbul, with its rich history, shall be the canvas upon which we paint our chaos."

Zoya, her gaze steady and deliberate, responded with words that carried the weight of their plan's significance in history.

"Indeed, Rashid. Our actions here will resonate through the annals of time. The chaos we compose shall be an opera, and the world will dance to its tune."

As they walked, Rashid and Zoya discussed their alliance as a "marriage of minds," a fusion of intellect and ambition designed to bring their vision to fruition. Their partnership was not born of chance but of a shared desire to shift the balance of power on a global scale.

Rashid's hand rested on a dossier, its contents containing their meticulously crafted plans. The dossier showcased their foresight and attention to detail, a testament to the careful planning that had brought them to this point. Zoya's intensity never wavered, her determination clear in every line of her face and every word she spoke. The black sedan continued its journey, now approaching the iconic Topkapi Palace, a symbol of historic grandeur contrasted against Obsidian Dawn's dark intentions. Rashid and Zoya contemplated the world's attention on their forthcoming event, knowing that their actions would forever alter the course of history.

They ascended the steps of the palace, and their plan unfolded like the silhouette of a predator against Istanbul's canvas. The stage was set for a history-altering narrative within the grand ballroom of Topkapi Palace, where the world's fate would swing by the strings, pulled by these two.

"Just a few more weeks to go, then we shall restore a new world order, one where the chaos becomes our greatest weapon. The world will bend to our will." Rashid pointed at the rest of the city from the stairs of the Topkapi Palace.

Zoya broke the silence too, her eyes full of darkness. "We're writing the destiny, Rashid. One that will rewrite the balance of power."

"And those who dare to stand against us will be swept aside by the tide we've set in motion."

Rashid's smile deepened as he turned his face to the palace, holding Zoya by the waist and saying, "In the grand ballroom of this Topkapi Palace, darling, our beloved Obsidian Dawn shall take over the world."

Chapter 5

Shadows and Steel

The common folk in Turkey were oblivious to Rashid's nefarious plans on his spindle of evil. Backed by his Egyptian sidekick Zoya, he wouldn't stop at anything. The Arab business tycoon and self-proclaimed philanthropist Rashid had used countless tactics of mass control, and his attacks would rarely be missed. He had gained a loyal following of naïve commoners who would pick a fight with anyone who took a dig at this Colossus of terror.

The most potent ammunition in his arsenal was control. His devilish agitprop and deceptive modus operandi had brainwashed the people of the world into recognizing him as a benevolent God, a higher moral authority, and the torchbearer of all the goodness in the world.

At his core, he was nothing short of a grifter. Now, he had a clear playing field before him. He would use his sham reputation to his advantage and launch an offensive unlike any other. With one push of a button, he would wipe out those he deemed obstructive in his path to glory.

Would the plan be executed, there'd be no one left to stand up to him, and then he would claim his supremacy.

While the people of Istanbul marveled at the magnificence of their country, they were naïve enough not to take heed of the possibility of something going wrong. At the same time, the defense officials of the world had gathered at the crossroads of the world. On the one hand, nightly partying and frolic infested the streets of Istanbul, and on the other hand, R&AW's professionals were hard at work. In the headquarters of India's Research and Analysis Wing, the tensions were high, but nothing came close to defeating the steely determination of the five people. Now, with Vikrant's added foresight and experience, they were a step closer to making the unholy plans of the Obsidian Dawn crash and burn, burying the likes of Zoya and Rashid in the trenches of history, never to be heard of again.

Vikrant's ability to smell things from afar, evaluating diverse options, and coming up with the right solutions had given the team an edge over their adversaries. His prowess was unbecoming of his age, and interestingly, it had little to do with him being gifted. Instead, it had more to do with his determination that traced its provenance in his love for humanity and the fiery hankering for vanquishing the devil on his own turf.

With Vikrant on board, their process of strategy was nothing less than a game of chess. Before someone could propose an idea, he would turn it down as his mind was fixated on how the Obsidian Dawn would counter their moves.

While Maya, Aisha and Arjun spoke with Vikrant, Sikandar, and Tony remained silent. They were the two senior faces in the lot, and they trusted Vikrant enough because of his professional exploits and accolades. Vikrant had managed to cultivate a loyal following within his department, and his reputation preceded him.

Finally, the two men walked over to the table where the other four people were seated with their laptops and tablets.

"We must anticipate their every move, guys," said Tony.

"We got this Tony, don't you worry," said Maya.

"Not so fast Maya. We shouldn't forget who we're up against," replied Tony.

"Rashid is one of the most formidable people I have ever seen," he added.

"Tony is right, guys. Rashid may be a rogue, but he knows how to play with minds," said Vikrant.

"He has so intelligently veiled himself under the disguise of heroism, and the worst part? The people trust him," said Maya.

"Poor people. They don't know what he's up to," said Aisha.

"What's even scary is that he believes utterly in the necessity of what he's doing. If he makes up his mind, he doesn't go to sleep until it is an ordained thing," said Sikandar.

Silence fell into the room. Every solitary soul surrounding the table delved into some deep thought. There was confusion, questions, and doubts in the minds of the people in the room.

The thought of taking on someone as extraordinary as Rashid was appallingly overwhelming. It was a mammoth task, arduous enough to make even the most resolute person doubt their gut. The typing had stopped, and the only cacophony colliding against their eardrums was the sound of the ceiling fan.

Sikandar rested backward in his revolving chair and stared at the ceiling. Tony was puffing one cigarette after another, hoping it would help him cool down. Arjun loosened his necktie, trying to breathe just a little.

Aisha was gazing at her feet with her fingers on her forehead and her elbows on the table. The silence elongated, and no one could utter a single syllable. Hopelessness was hovering over R&AW's headquarters. It was about to enter through the vents like an unholy spirit, but Maya spoke up, breaking the silence.

"Guys, let's not lose hope."

"Alright, I understand who we are up against, and I know the chances of success are sparse, but we have to give it our best," she added.

Maya was a young digital enthusiast, and her experience didn't match up to the likes of Tony and Sikandar. However, she had sensed that her team was on the verge of losing hope, and that is exactly what she feared more than losing to Rashid and Zoya.

She wanted her comrades to fight till the last drop of their blood, and she was more than ready to do just that.

"Guys, we will make their digital efforts backfire. Even if they move like phantoms in the night, they won't be able to pass through our controls," she added.

"I know that Maya is a little too optimistic, but if we click together, not allow any slip-ups, and stick to the plan, we can all just make it," said Aisha.

"Listen guys, I understand that this mission is easier said than done, but something inside me tells me we are about to write history," said Maya.

"Imagine for a brief moment if we could pull this off, we will go down in history as the vanguards that unveiled and vanquished a great villain," she added. Maya's words had transformed into a borderline motivational speech. Considering her age, such words of wisdom were unexpected from her. As Maya stopped speaking, she realized that everyone was looking at her. There was deafening silence once again, but this time it wasn't the silence of hopelessness.

Sikandar looked at Tony, and the two burst out laughing. They were followed by the team.

"Very funny, guys," said Maya with a semi-stern tone.

"Oh my God, Maya, you have something going on there. I wonder why you don't make it to the parliament," said Aisha.

In the middle of a heated brainstorming session, that is exactly what was needed; a laugh. At first, Maya stared at everyone as if she was planning to eat them alive. Her face was red with fury, but when she realized that no one was willing to stop, she, too, burst out laughing.

The laughter had given them some outlet, an opportunity to vent. It helped them replenish their strength to keep going, a strength that was exhausted only a few minutes ago.

"I think we should step outside only for a bit. What do you guys think," asked Sikandar.

"Damn right, comrade. We need some fresh air," replied Tony.

"Let's discuss the remaining stuff over some coffee," said Vikrant.

The team left their seats and headed for the breakroom.

"Ok, guys, we must trust our skills and our expertise, but we mustn't write off the foresight the Obsidian Dawn possesses," said Arjun.

"Disruption is the biggest weapon in their toolkit, and that is where our work begins," said Sikandar.

"We must keep a close eye on their activities," said Aisha.

"Our preparations should be ready before they could make a move," she added.

"I am sure they will make a mistake, and we mustn't let that mistake go to waste," said Vikrant.

"No matter how cunning the culprit is, he is bound to make at least one mistake, and that mistake will work to our advantage," added Vikrant.

"That's right! Rashid is the most notorious criminal in the world, and the fact that the world trusts him will work to our advantage," said Tony.

"I'm listening, but how exactly will that happen?" asked Sikandar inquisitively.

"Look, guys. Rashid knows how blindly people trust him. He won't expect anyone from the crowd to get in his way, and while he may expect some intervention, his overconfidence will keep him from realizing the extent of resistance," said Tony.

"Alright, we need cameras in every corner of the venue. We need to split strategically but keep your GPS and mouthpieces handy. In this mission, communication and coordination are key, and we can't afford a mix-up," said Vikrant.

Now, the team had a direction, and the once vague target had become clearer. From that point on, it was a game of nerves. The belligerent to keep their composure and not give the game away would end up victorious.

Chapter 6

Shadows of Intrigue and the Grand Ballroom

As the sedan glided forward with the dossier in Rashid's hand, the grandeur of Topkapi Palace came into view, its historic significance a stark contrast to the Obsidian Dawn's malevolent intentions. The opulence of the palace was a striking backdrop, a testament to the scale of their ambitions.

"The world will watch," Rashid mused, his voice tinged with a sense of theatricality.

Zoya's gaze shifted from the Palace to Rashid and she smiled sinisterly. "And they'll bear witness to a new era—a world reshaped by our hands."

As they moved closer to the palace, the Obsidian Dawn's plan unfurled like a predator's silhouette against the canvas of Istanbul. Within the grand ballroom's embrace, Rashid and Zoya's narrative would intertwine with the fate of nations, forever altering the course of history.

The main street led to the palace's main entrance, secured with a massive marble gate. The palace was huge, with four consecutive courtyards surrounded by high walls. Each courtyard served different purposes and was separated by a gate that incrementally restricted entry, culminating in the most-private third and fourth courtyards.

Zoya and Rashid entered The Gate of Felicity, the entrance to the third courtyard of the palace where the ball was held. The ballroom of the Topkapi Palace glittered. The walls were like gold and the lights shone like pearls against them. The room was six hundred feet long by four hundred feet wide. Its ceiling stretched up another two hundred feet above their heads. Dozens of glittering large crystal chandeliers hung from the ceiling, sending a lovely diffused golden light over the ballroom's occupants.

Zoya wore a flowing, elaborately jeweled ball gown of the most beautiful shade of emerald. The smell of roses, hyacinth, and jasmine flowed in the garden outside the palace. Low chatters could be heard when Rashid, in his simple black suit, darker than the night sky, stood beside Zoya.

Within the opulent surroundings of the grand ballroom, Rashid Al Mansoor and Zoya Ilayat moved with calculated grace, their elegant attire concealing the underlying tension that hung heavy in the air. Their conversation, laced with cryptic hints and veiled meanings, spoke of a plan to orchestrate chaos and disrupt the illusion of normalcy and peace.

Rashid leaned in close to Zoya, his voice a low, deliberate murmur. "Zoya, time has come to set our plan in motion. The world must see what lies beneath the façade."

Zoya, her demeanor poised and enigmatic, replied in kind. "Rashid, the illusions they cling to must crumble, revealing the truth that has remained hidden for far too long."

As they conversed amidst the swirl of dancers and the shimmering chandeliers, those nearby sensed an undercurrent of intrigue and danger.

Rashid glanced around the ballroom, his gaze meeting Zoya's briefly, and then he continued, "The key players are in position, and our network is ready. The chaos we create will expose their vulnerabilities and force them to confront the reality they've been avoiding." She nodded in agreement, her eyes reflecting the gravity of their intentions. "Yes, Rashid, but we must be cautious. The forces we are up against are powerful, and they will not yield easily."

As the music started, the couples took to the dance floor. They swirled and twirled to the rhythm of the music. The sound of the orchestra filled the air, and the chandeliers overhead cast a glow over the room.

Rashid leaned toward Zoya, "Shall we?" He extended his hand.

Zoya took a deep breath and straightened her back, feeling her flowing gown and the soft fabric of her gloves. "Gladly." She placed her hand into his and they began to dance, moving gracefully across the floor.

To avoid suspicion, they decided to just enjoy the ball. They were brilliant in being inconspicuous, blending in, and avoiding suspicious eyes. So, they continued dancing around the people.

Zoya followed Rashid's lead. They spun in circles and shuffled their feet to the slow, rhythmic music. It was just like paradise, but even more when their eyes met.

Suddenly, the music changed its pace, this time slow and relaxing. Rashid smiled at Zoya slightly and pulled her body closer to his. She blushed and his smile only grew bigger.

After some time, they ended up in a secluded area near the windows, where no one could hear them.

Rashid cast subtle looks around the room to find anyone spying on them, but there was no one, at least not at the moment. They went up the stone stairs, the spiral shape of them somewhat amusing. The railing was decorated with moonflower and evening primroses.

"So, I want to treat you after our work is done, and one of my friends has a champagne cellar. Drink with me?" he asked politely, a flirtatious smile on his face as he waited for her response.

"Since you asked so nicely, I will gladly accept," she said with a giggle.

***

Back at the R&AW base, Tony stood in front of a large screen displaying the surveillance images inside the palace. He finally spotted them.

He addressed the team gathered around him, his tone serious and determined, "Listen up, everyone. These two," Tony pointed to Rashid and Zoya, "are the key players, the architects of the chaos that threatens the world, the linchpins behind the Obsidian Dawn. Keep your eyes on the screen; I was damn sure they will be here and it's easy for us now that we have seen their faces."

Sikandar stepped forward. "We can't underestimate them. They may have a network of operatives at their disposal. But we have something they don't: the knowledge of their plan."

Aisha added, "We've been analyzing their communications and movements. There are cracks in their plan, weaknesses we can exploit if we act swiftly."

Maya leaned forward. "We need to stay ahead of their moves. They're playing a high-stakes game, but we have the advantage of knowing their intentions. Let's focus on disarming their network."

Arjun laid a map of the palace on the table and looked at his team, "Our mission is clear: disrupt their operations, expose their vulnerabilities, and dismantle Obsidian Dawn."

As the team huddled around the screen, they began to strategize, brainstorming ways to exploit weaknesses in Obsidian Dawn's plan. Arjun rubbed his temple. "We'll hit them where they least expect it, disrupt their operations from within. But the question is, how?!"

Rashid and Zoya came back into the ballroom and blended in with the guests again. Rashid leaned in closer to Zoya, and spoke in a hushed tone, "The world is in dire need of change, Zoya. Our plan will dismantle the foundations of their false reality and pave the way for a new dawn, an era where the truth prevails."

Zoya's expression remained resolute. "Yes, Rashid, but we must be prepared for the consequences. The forces we challenge are powerful, and they will stop at nothing to maintain their illusions." She took a sip from her wine glass.

"Don't worry, my dear, they are incapable of overpowering us." He grinned, and continued, "The world must witness the discord we unleash, for it is only through chaos that their illusions can be shattered."

They kept talking in enigmatic tones, their eyes focused on the crowd. "Our mission will pave the way for a new dawn, a paradigm shift that will birth our ideology."

As the music swelled and the couples gracefully twirled across the polished floor, a man in a black suit approached them and extended his hand with a courteous smile. "Madam, would you do me the honor of sharing this dance with me?" He held a glint of admiration in his eyes.

Zoya, who was deeply immersed in her plans, felt frustrated as she did not want her attention to be diverted. But to blend in, she knew she had to have the dance. She placed her hand in his. "Of course, I would be delighted."

The man led her onto the dance floor, and they began to dance. As they waltzed, Zoya kept her eyes on the ballroom. She wondered if this man was someone who had come to sabotage their plan, but she couldn't come to a conclusion.

The man leaned in slightly and spoke softly. "I couldn't help but notice your beauty. It's not often one encounters someone as intriguing as you."

"Events like these often hide the most intriguing stories, don't you think?" Zoya smirked as he bent her backward in his arms.

The man's smile widened. "Indeed, they do. But sometimes, it's the stories that remain untold that hold the most intrigue. The people and their agendas."

"So you're a talker, huh?" She smiled as he twirled her around.

The music came to an end, and they both bowed to each other. "It was lovely dancing with you." He gently pecked her hand and led her back to Rashid.

"Was that guy up to something?" Rashid placed his wine glass back on the table. "At first, I was doubting him as well. But he seems to be an admirer of my beauty." She shrugged.

"All right, all right." Rashid chuckled, "There are plenty of admirers in this ballroom; I can't let you dance with each one of them."

As they continued their flirtatious talk, the diplomats from around the world started filling in the ballroom which caught Zoya's and Rashid's attention. Their faces quickly shifted from laughing to serious as they stared at the men who had just entered the ballroom. The delegates gathered around a long, polished table with microphones and flags of their respective countries.

As the diplomats took their seats, the Turkish president addressed the assembly. "Ladies and gentlemen, we have gathered here to chart a new course for our world. The events that have transpired recently have exposed vulnerabilities in our global system. It is time for unity and collaboration to mend those rifts. We must put aside our differences and seek common ground. The pursuit of global stability is not the task of one nation but of humanity as a whole." Throughout the meeting, the importance of cooperation, diplomacy, and compromise was emphasized. As the speech continued, Zoya and Rashid exchanged glances with each other, knowing that they were about to destroy this shitshow.

Chapter 7

Shadows Unveiled - Bonds and Purpose

Tony, Sikandar, and Aisha gathered around a holographic projection table. The table projected a three-dimensional map of the palace's layout, with various points marked for reference. The ambient hum of machinery and the urgency in the air were palpable.

Tony leaned forward, studying the holographic map. "We need to regroup our teams and secure the exits. I don't know what their plan is yet, but we need to be ready for anything."

"I've accessed the palace's security feed. They tried, but we have their faces now. I found out their car's plate number as well; we will track them if they try to run."

"Our top priority is to ensure the safety of the attendees. Once we've accounted for everyone, we can focus on tracking down those responsible." Aisha raised her eyes.

Tony tapped the projection table, highlighting the locations of their undercover agents. "Our teams are in position. We must apprehend the culprits before they slip away."

"We've got Zoya and Rashid, but we need to find their partners." Sikandar's fingers danced over a holographic keyboard, pulling up facial recognition algorithms. "I'm cross-referencing the assailants' faces with known databases. We may get lucky and find a match and find out where these roaches are lurking." Aisha glanced at her wrist communicator, receiving updates from their field operatives. "Our teams have secured all exits. No one leaves this place until we've conducted thorough checks. The criminals won't escape." In another part of the Intelligence Bureau, Maya and Arjun found themselves in a dimly lit room, surrounded by stacks of intelligence reports and surveillance footage. Their mission: to unravel the motives and mysteries behind the Obsidian Dawn.

Maya scrutinized a stack of documents with meticulous precision. "Arjun," she began, her voice tinged with determination, "we need to find the threads that connect these seemingly unrelated events. The Obsidian Dawn is elusive, but they can't hide from us forever."

Arjun, a seasoned analyst known for his perseverance, nodded in agreement. "You're right, Maya. We can't afford to let them slip through our fingers."

As they delved deeper into the reports, each piece of evidence they uncovered was like a puzzle piece, fitting into the larger picture of the Obsidian Dawn's activities.

"I'm exhausted. Shall we take a break for a moment? Maybe that will clear our heads and help us think better," Arjun suggested.

"Oh yes, I'd love that." Maya was relieved.

Seeking a moment of respite at R&AW's secure base, the operatives stepped away from the relentless analysis for a brief moment. They sat in a quiet corner, sipping on cups of tea, their faces etched with determination.

"Maya," Arjun said, "it's not just about defeating the Obsidian Dawn. It's about combating an ideology of chaos and creating a more stable world for future generations."

"Absolutely!" Maya continued, her voice filled with conviction. "Our responsibility is not just to uncover the truth; it's to shape the world's future. To create a world where chaos is not the prevailing force, but stability, justice, and hope."

Arjun nodded in agreement. "And it starts with our unwavering determination. Our unity in the face of chaos is our greatest strength."

As they spoke, their reflections deepened. They discussed the importance of stability on a global scale, the consequences of chaos, and the profound impact their work had on the lives of countless people around the world.

Maya's eyes shone with a fierce resolve. "We are the ones who must combat chaos. We will confront the Obsidian Dawn's ideology head-on, and we will shape a world that is more stable, just, and resilient."

As they stood silent for a while, Arjun's mind flashed with something.

Maya noticed the change in his demeanor and asked, concern etching her features, "Arjun, what's wrong?"

Arjun's voice trembled as he replied, "Oh my God, Maya, I know what they're going to do. They're going to poison the air."

Maya's eyes widened as she absorbed the gravity of his words. "What? How do you know that, Arjun?"

Arjun quickly retrieved his tablet and pulled up a surveillance footage feed from the summit at the palace.

He played back a section of the video, his finger pointing to a group of individuals who were transporting large cylinders.

“Look here,” he said, “Zoya and Rashid are seen with the laborers loading the cylinders in the van outside the warehouse, and now,” he opened another footage, “look here - those same cylinders are lined up at the back door of the Palace.”

“You think they’re planning to release a gas.”

Arjun nodded gravely. “It’s a possibility. And if they do, it could be even more devastating. We need to alert the security teams immediately.”

Arjun picked up his secure satellite phone and dialed Sikandar’s number.

“Yes, Arjun? Found something?”

Arjun wasted no time. “Sikandar, I’ve just uncovered a critical piece of information. It looks like the Obsidian Dawn is planning to release a gas into the air at the summit. We have to act fast.”

“Are you sure, Arjun?”

Arjun nodded. “I’ve reviewed the footage from the palace, and it’s unmistakable. They’ve brought cylinders, and those same cylinders were taken in the palace.”

Sikandar's fingers flew over his keyboard as he processed the information. "Alright, Arjun. Let's not waste any more time. We need to inform the Turkish Police immediately and coordinate our efforts to prevent this disaster." Sikandar informed Aisha and Tony and made the call to the Turkish Police. After a few intense minutes, Sikandar hung up the phone and turned to Tony, a determined look in his eyes. "The Turkish Police have been alerted. They're taking it seriously, and they're mobilizing their response teams to secure the cylinders and ensure the safety of the summit attendees."

"Listen up, everyone," Tony declared, his words cutting through the noise of analysts and operatives. "We're going to Turkey to stop the Obsidian Dawn and bring those bastards down."

He continued. "We've alerted the Turkish Police, but we can't leave anything to chance. We need to be on the ground. We'll use every resource at our disposal to track down their operatives and dismantle their plans. There will be no room for error."

Tony locked eyes with each of his colleagues, a determined fire in his gaze. "Let's move out. Time is of the essence, and we can't afford to waste a single second."

***

They sipped champagne as the Turkish president took the stage to deliver his opening remarks. The room was filled with chatter and applause as he continued his speech.

Zoya leaned closer to Rashid, her voice barely above a whisper. "Rashid, it's time. Are you sure everything is set?"

Rashid nodded discreetly. "The poison is in place, and our companions are ready to release the gas on your signal."

Zoya smirked and clinked her glass with Rashid's. "To a new world order."

They both took a sip of their champagne.

As the president droned on, Zoya and Rashid began to mockingly discuss their sinister plan under the guise of casual conversation.

Zoya chuckled softly. "You know, Rashid, this summit is supposed to bring peace and unity, but I can't help but think that chaos and confusion will serve our interests better."

Rashid feigned innocence. "Oh, Zoya, you're always so pessimistic. Maybe the world needs a little chaos to find its true order."

Just then, Zoya discreetly pressed a small button on her wristwatch, sending a signal to their unseen companions. In an unassuming utility closet nearby, operatives released a colorless, odorless gas into the ventilation system.

Zoya and Rashid took one last sip of their champagne and calmly made their way towards the exit.

The people at the summit didn't notice the wisp of smoke curling out from beneath the vents. Just as the president was delivering a key point of his speech, a man in the audience cried out for help. His voice was filled with desperation, and his words were barely discernible amidst the commotion.

"Help! Someone, please, help me!"

The president halted mid-sentence, his brow furrowing in confusion. The audience's attention swiftly shifted from the eloquent speech to the chaos that had erupted in their midst. People began coughing and covering their mouths, their faces contorting with distress. In a couple of minutes, the gas turned into a torrent pouring around the doors. Those standing nearby were almost completely obscured by the white cloud, and a woman let out a small scream as the sudden shift in the wind sent the plume billowing in her direction.

People started to cough; some spluttered and cried out for help while others dropped to the ground.

Panic spread like wildfire. VIPs and diplomats exchanged worried glances, their curiosity about the unfolding drama overriding their initial enthusiasm for the president's address. Whispers and alarmed murmurs filled the room.

The president, his speech momentarily forgotten, leaned forward to get a better view of the source of the commotion. He was met with a disconcerting sight: a man in the middle of the audience, clutching his chest and struggling to breathe. His face had turned a pallid shade of gray, and tears streamed down his cheeks as he gasped for air.

Security personnel rushed to the stricken man's side, pushing through the bewildered crowd. Medical professionals in the audience began to assist, checking his vitals and administering aid as best they could in the rapidly deteriorating situation.

As the chaos intensified, the president stepped away from the podium, a look of concern etched across his face. The once-attentive audience was now divided between watching the unfolding medical emergency and casting fearful glances around the room to identify the source of the affliction that had befallen them.

In the midst of the commotion, a sharp-eyed security officer, scanning the room for signs of trouble, noticed something alarming. His gaze fixed on the ornate vents near the ceiling. A faint, eerie haze was seeping from the vents, like wisps of a malevolent specter. He alerted his colleagues, shouting over the mounting tumult, "Look up there! Gas! The air is poisoned!"

The revelation sent shockwaves through the security team, who immediately understood the gravity of the situation. Their training had prepared them for many scenarios, but this was a crisis of unforeseen proportions.

They sprang into action, prioritizing the safety of the VIPs above all else. Shouts of "Evacuate the room!" and "Protect the dignitaries!" echoed through the ballroom as security officials rushed to form a protective perimeter around the world leaders and high-ranking diplomats.

VIPs, initially paralyzed by shock, were now guided by the determined security personnel. They were ushered toward the exits, with guards forming a human shield around them. Panicked whispers filled the air as the attendees began to grasp the gravity of the situation.

They guided the VIPs out of the ballroom one by one, ensuring their safety as they exited through the grand doors.

Amid the chaos and panic that had engulfed the grand ballroom, there was one small but crucial detail that went unnoticed by Zoya and Rashid: a blocked vent near the podium.

It was a stroke of fate or perhaps a twist of luck for those who were present inside that a maintenance worker's tool chest had obstructed the vent closest to the podium. Unbeknownst to anyone in the room, a wrench had fallen from the chest and lodged itself securely into the vent, acting as an unwitting barrier. As the invisible, poisonous gas permeated the ballroom, it spread unevenly. Attendees who were closer to other vents began to experience the debilitating effects of the toxin, which gave time for the security officials to figure out what was happening as they were standing mere feet from the blocked vent.

The blocked vent had, in essence, acted as a shield, delaying the arrival of the deadly gas. It was as though fate had chosen to spare those closest to the center of the event.

It took about five minutes before hazy blue flashing lights emerged around the corner, indicating that help was on its way. Firefighters climbed into cumbersome protection suits with full breathing apparatus. They moved from victim to victim, checking who could be saved and who was beyond help.

Chapter 8

Istanbul - A Journey of Unity and Inspiration

The team had reached Istanbul before the gas was released in the ballroom. In the meantime, as they stepped on Istanbul's soil, the city captivated them with the colors, sounds, and smells that greeted them at every turn. They passed by the Grand Bazaar, a labyrinthine marketplace. Its arched doorways and domed ceilings showcased intricate mosaics.

Shopkeepers beckoned with a warm smile, offering handmade rugs, ornate lamps, and spices that filled the air with a fragrant symphony.

The team also passed by the street art adorning the walls and live music spilling out from cosy cafes. Here, they witnessed the creative spirit of the city's youth and their determination to express themselves freely.

As the car stopped at the small family-owned restaurant tucked away in a quiet alley, Tony addressed his team, "Everyone, we are going to meet our undercover agents in Istanbul. We will be given our weapons there."

As they entered the charming eatery, the restaurant was cozy and inviting, with tables adorned in checkered tablecloths and the aroma of freshly baked bread and simmering spices filling the air.

Just as they settled in their seats, a discreet nod from the waiter signaled the arrival of someone familiar. Two individuals, dressed inconspicuously, entered the restaurant and took a seat at a nearby table. A subtle exchange of glances confirmed the identities of both parties, and it was clear that the agents had chosen this unassuming restaurant for a reason. The team understood that this was not a typical rendezvous spot. Still, Istanbul's labyrinthine streets offered anonymity and safety. Just then, a friendly, middle-aged man with a warm smile approached their table. He introduced himself as Hasan, the owner of the restaurant. "Welcome to our humble establishment," he said. "I hope you enjoy your meal tonight. What can I bring you?"

They all placed their orders. After they placed their orders, they couldn't help but notice that a waiter, Hasan, seemed to linger near their table as if he had something more to say. Finally, he leaned in, lowering his voice.

"I couldn't help but overhear your conversation about your time in Istanbul," he said. "It's a city full of surprises, isn't it?"

"It is a city full of surprises, isn't it." This was the code word they had to use so they understood that they were undercover agents.

The team exchanged glances. Maya replied, "Yes, it truly is. We've been amazed by the stories and experiences we've encountered here."

Just then, a group of people at a nearby table stood up to leave. They were discreetly carrying small parcels wrapped in plain brown paper. As they passed by the team's table, Hasan nodded to them with a knowing smile.

One of the individuals from the departing group, a woman with a subtle air of secrecy about her, leaned in and whispered to the team, "Enjoy your meal, and remember that Istanbul has more layers than you can imagine." With that, she discreetly handed a small envelope to Tony before walking away. The team exchanged surprised glances as they watched the group of people vanish into the crowd outside. Tony quickly opened the envelope to find a message written in code, along with a USB drive.

Hasan leaned in again, his voice even lower. "Istanbul has a way of revealing its secrets to those who seek them," he said cryptically. "Enjoy your meal, my friends."

Over a delicious meal of traditional Turkish cuisine, the team engaged in casual conversation with the agents, using coded language and subtle gestures to exchange information. They discussed the progress of their mission, shared critical updates, and confirmed their next steps.

One of them slid the bag underneath the table towards Tony containing a grappling hook, 100' rope, Pistol, handcuffs, black suits, and a walkie-talkie wrist mic. All the things that they needed to catch them. But one thing was still missing, "Where's the car?"

"Don't worry, two cars are waiting for you outside the restaurant." One of them slid the car key in front of him.

When the owner of the restaurant arrived to ask for their feedback, Sikandar complimented them. "Ah, the food! I've never tasted anything quite like this before."

"Yeah, that's amazing. I've never thought Turkish food could be so amazing. Thank you, sir, for such an amazing meal." Aisha smiled. The owner shared the story of how his family had been serving generations of locals and travelers alike. He spoke of the challenges they had faced, from economic downturns to political upheavals, and how they had persevered through it all, nourishing both body and soul.

"You are so welcoming. What's your name, sir?" Aisha cupped her face and leaned on the table.

"Ahh it's Mehmet ma'am." He smiled.

As they sipped the Turkish tea, they struck up a conversation with Mehmet, the owner, a kind-hearted man who had lived in Istanbul his entire life. His eyes sparkled with pride as he spoke about his city's rich heritage.

Mehmet shared tales of Istanbul's many transformations, from its days as Byzantium to Constantinople and eventually Istanbul. He spoke of the city's resilience through centuries of conquests, empires rising and falling, and the enduring spirit of its people. His words painted a vivid picture of a city that had weathered the storms of history, emerging stronger each time.

He regaled them with stories of his family's heritage, passed down through generations. He spoke of his grandparents' struggles during difficult times and how they had managed to keep their restaurant alive.

"I was born and raised in this city, and let me tell you, Istanbul has seen its fair share of challenges. From the days of my grandparents, through wars and political changes, the city has always endured."

Maya leaned in. "It must have been quite a journey. What do you think is the secret to Istanbul's endurance?"

Mehmet paused. "The secret, my dear friends, is unity. Istanbul is a melting pot of cultures and religions, and it's in our diversity that we find our strength. We've learned to live side by side, respecting each other's differences. This unity is what makes us resilient."

Sikandar was amused. "That's truly inspiring. Can you share a specific story of resilience or hope that you've witnessed in your lifetime?"

Mehmet nodded. "Certainly. During one of the toughest times in recent history, when political unrest shook our city, I saw neighbors helping neighbors, sharing what little they had. It was a reminder that even in the darkest of times, there is light to be found in the kindness of people."

"That's beautiful, Mehmet." Maya smiled at him.

"Umm, guys, we are getting late." Tony reminded. "Mehmet, it was great to meet you, but we have to be somewhere now." He smiled.

"Yes, yes, sure." Mehmet smiled warmly. "It was a pleasure meeting you."

As they got out of the office, Tony passed one of the car keys to Arjun and Maya. "Arjun, Maya, this is it. Our mission to find Rashid and Zoya depends on us. We need to split up and keep an eye on the palace."

"Understood, Tony. We'll be watching over the palace." Arjun nodded.

"We won't let you down, Tony. We'll find them."

"I'll go with them, Tony. They would need help." Aisha stepped forward. "All right, Aisha. Sikandar and I will be at the Galata Bridge. If they get out of your sight, then we will be here. I'm pretty sure their escape route will include the bridge."

"Okay then, we're leaving for the Palace. Shit's gonna get real now." Arjun smirked as he shrugged his shoulders. "Ladies." He opened the car door and gestured for the girls to sit. "Hasta la Vista." He waved goodbye to Sikandar and Tony and hit the engine on the road.

As they left, Tony and Sikandar drove to the Galata Bridge.

***

Under the dawn's soft, golden glow, Tony and Sikandar stood side by side on the Galata Bridge, a place where the past and present of Istanbul converged. The sun slowly crept above the horizon, casting a warm light on the city's historic districts.

Tony gazed at the view, "This place is so beautiful. It's so sad that we are on a mission here and not a vacation." He chuckled.

Sikandar nodded. "Yeah, I was thinking the same. The blend of Byzantine, Ottoman, and modern influences is unlike anywhere else in the world."

They watched as small fishing boats glided gracefully beneath the bridge, their occupants casting nets into the shimmering waters of the Golden Horn. The calls of seagulls echoed overhead. "We're not just here to complete a mission, Sikandar. We're here to protect this rich history, to ensure that future generations can walk these ancient streets and marvel at the same wonders we see today. I don't know what they plan to do after they release the gas in the ballroom, but all I can say is that they intend the destruction of this country."

"Don't worry, we won't let that happen." Sikandar gently pressed Tony's shoulder to ensure that they would stop the ones who threatened to cause chaos.

"Tony, Sultanahmet Square is just a nine-minute walk from here. I always wanted to go there. And we have to wait for a long time; Arjun will contact us if they will see Rashid and Zoya. In the meantime, I'd like to visit the place. I'll be back soon."

"I'll go with you; we will be back in time. And besides, everything is a step ahead in our plan, so there is plenty of time."

As Tony and Sikandar went to Sultanahmet Square, they were enveloped with a fusion of languages, colors, and laughter. The locals and tourists and the aroma of freshly roasted chestnuts with the sweet scent of Turkish delight enticed passersby to sample the culinary delights.

Sikandar admired the landmarks: "These buildings have witnessed centuries of change, yet they stand tall, embodying the city's enduring spirit."

As they were still there, Arjun contacted them, "It's time for action, guys." He said.

"We are ready," Tony replied.

"We must head back to the bridge," As soon as Tony informed Sikandar, they rushed out of Sultanahmet Square to take their positions at the bridge. Meanwhile, Rashid's and Zoya's sinister plan was about to take full effect in the palace and would lead to a showdown in the busy streets of Istanbul.

Chapter 9

Pursuit and Confrontation: A Dance of Danger

Rashid and Zoya's plan to release the poisonous gas had marvelously failed; thanks to the shrewd expertise displayed by Arjun and the team, they had managed to get everyone out alive, though a few, including the president, were intoxicated and had passed out from the fumes. As Arjun and Maya guided those overcome by the gas to safety, Rashid and Zoya took advantage of the confusion. They slipped away, melting into the shadows once more. The labyrinthine alleys of Istanbul provided the perfect escape route for the cunning operatives.

"Tony! Sikandar! They've escaped; Maya and I are rescuing the delegates with the help of the Turkish police. You need to go after Zoya and Rashid!" urged Arjun.

"On it," Tony said with resolve, gesturing to Arjun to prepare for the chase.

In the distance, police sirens and the blaring ambulances could be heard as they rushed to the Palace. The mission had evolved from capturing Zoya and Rashid to a full-scale operation to neutralize the threat posed by the Obsidian Dawn.

With the Turkish Police as their allies, the agents moved swiftly and decisively through the city, following every lead and piece of intelligence they had gathered. The clock was ticking, and they knew that time was of the essence. Their resolve would be tested as they navigated the treacherous path that lay ahead. As Tony and Sikandar pursued their elusive targets through the labyrinthine streets and bustling bazaars of Istanbul, their quest became a whirlwind of determination and evasion. The Obsidian Dawn, a shadowy organization that had long eluded their grasp, was within reach, and the agents were determined to seize this opportunity.

The sun dipped low on the horizon, casting long, dramatic shadows on the cobblestone streets. The city, a tapestry of rich history and vibrant culture, held the secrets they sought. Tony and Sikandar had received a valuable tip from their confidential informant, a thread of hope in the complex web of their mission. The informant had pointed them in the direction of the Obsidian Dawn's operatives, Zoya and Rashid, who were rumoured to be hidden somewhere within the old city.

This tip served as a beacon, drawing them closer and closer to their targets. The agents recognized that capturing Zoya and Rashid would be a significant breakthrough in dismantling the Obsidian Dawn, the criminal syndicate that had evaded justice for far too long. As the sun kissed the horizon, a sense of urgency infused their every step.

Their preparation had been meticulous, the product of weeks of gathering intelligence. They had familiarized themselves with the convoluted network of narrow alleys and bazaars that composed Istanbul's historic district. The city, with its complex web of various cultures and influences, was a puzzle with countless hidden corners, and Tony and Sikandar had resolved to master it.

However, as they pressed forward, it became evident that their adversaries, Zoya and Rashid, were astoundingly well-prepared. It was as if they could predict their every move, always ten steps ahead. Their pursuit of the elusive operatives began in earnest, the agents relying on their well-honed training, heightened senses, and the knowledge that every shadow concealed a potential threat.

The convoluted alleys of Istanbul seemed to have a life of their own, twisting and turning, creating countless hiding spots for those who wished to remain hidden. As Tony and Sikandar stealthily navigated the winding paths, their footsteps echoed softly against the ancient stones. The city itself became a silent observer, aware of the high-stakes chase unfolding within its historic heart.

Suddenly, a glimpse of a familiar silhouette appeared up ahead. It was Zoya, her ebony hair flowing in the wind as she moved like a ghost through the shadows. Sikandar signalled to Tony, and they quickened their pace, veering out of sight, hoping to remain unnoticed. Zoya, however, seemed to sense their presence, her own instincts sharp as a blade. The chase had officially begun.

Then, in a twist of fate, Rashid materialized seemingly out of thin air, blocking the path ahead of Tony and Sikandar. His dark eyes gleamed with a sinister resolve, knowing that the narrow alley had become a dead end, leaving the agents trapped.

"Take a good look, you two," Rashid mocked, his voice dripping with a chilling confidence. "We won't be with you for long."

Tony, unshaken, responded with determination, "You won't get away with this; your plan of killing all the delegates with the gas failed; count your days." Rashid and Zoya, who thought they had been successful in their sinister plot, looked at each other in dismay; their cunning plan had fallen flat. A tense, silent standoff unfolded in that dimly lit alley, where the balance of power teetered on a precipice. Tony and Sikandar knew they were facing formidable adversaries, masters of evasion tactics and subterfuge. It was a battle of wits, a chess match played out amidst the treacherous streets of Istanbul.

Suddenly, the silence was shattered by a deafening explosion at the base of the Galata Tower, a historic landmark that dominated the skyline. The ground trembled, and the sound of the explosion reverberated through the ancient walls around them. Tony and Sikandar were thrown to the ground, disoriented by the blast. The commotion served as the perfect distraction, allowing Zoya and Rashid to slip away.

When Tony and Sikander regained their bearings, they realized that the Obsidian Dawn had eluded them once again and was on the run. Sikandar's sense of urgency kicked in. "They couldn't have gotten far; get up and dust yourself off. We have a mission to complete!"

Tony and Sikandar quickly regrouped, adrenaline surging through their veins. They gave chase once more, determined to close in on Zoya and Rashid. As they pursued their targets through the winding streets, it became evident that this mission had evolved into a perilous game of cat and mouse, with each step they took posing a calculated risk.

The operatives seemed to anticipate their every move, leading them through a maze of uncertainty. It was an exhilarating but dangerous pursuit, with the tension palpable in the air. The chase became a dangerous gambit where one wrong move could tip the balance. Amidst the ever-changing streets of Istanbul, where each alley held imminent danger, Tony and Sikandar's focus remained unwavering. Their synchronicity was like a well-practised ballet, a testament to their years of partnership. But Zoya and Rashid, their elusive adversaries, moved with a grace and agility that made the pursuit even more challenging.

Tony's gaze shifted from one shadowy corner to the next; his instincts honed to a razor's edge. He knew that capturing Zoya and Rashid could unravel the intricate web of criminal activities orchestrated by the Obsidian Dawn. The weight of their mission pressed on his shoulders, but he refused to let it deter him. Every step he took was a substantial risk and a possible wrong move in a very treacherous game.

The narrow alleys seemed to conspire with their adversaries, twisting and turning, offering countless hiding places. The agents remained vigilant, every sense sharpened, as they followed the ever-shifting trail in what appeared to be a relentless pursuit.

With every twist and turn, Tony and Sikandar knew that the fate of an international criminal syndicate hung in the balance. Their pursuit continued, their hearts beating in sync as they darted frantically through Istanbul's narrow streets, now an arena, with each alleyway an unforeseen trap. Yet they both moved with a sense of unison that bordered on telepathic, as if they were two bodies united by one soul. Tony's eyes remained fixed on their quarry, his mind a tangled web of calculations. "We're almost there. Don't lose focus." Sikandar's voice carried an edge of urgency. "They're leading us into a trap. Be prepared." The tension hung in the air like a thick fog, the outcome of this case uncertain. They had let the operatives slip through their fingers like butter; the mission had escalated into a dangerous game. The operatives seemed to anticipate their moves, leading them through a maze of uncertainty. As they navigated the streets, which now began to morph into a maze, Tony and Sikandar were adamant, with the future of the world in their hands.

The escalating tension and adrenaline reached a fever pitch as Tony and Sikandar closed in on their elusive targets. The streets of Istanbul had led them to this moment, to a climactic showdown where the outcome of their mission would be determined. Shadows of conflicting ideologies loomed large, their own commitment to justice pitted against the ruthless determination of the Obsidian Dawn.

With each heartbeat, they drew nearer to the epicentre of their pursuit. Tony's senses were razor-sharp, every muscle coiled with anticipation. Sikandar moved like a shadow, vigilant and unwavering. The chase had been relentless, but they were determined not to let the elusive operatives slip away again.

It had led them to a dilapidated courtyard hidden deep within the heart of the timeless district. The ancient stones beneath their feet seemed to whisper tales of a bygone era, a place where history and secrets had been buried. The courtyard, bathed in moonlight, took on an eerie, ethereal quality.

As they approached, the stage was set for a final confrontation. Shadows danced on the walls, casting ghostly silhouettes that seemed to echo the journey of chaos and order that had brought them here. Meanwhile, Zoya and Rashid stood ready, their expressions a mix of determination and defiance. The Obsidian Dawn's agents flanked them, a formidable force cloaked in anonymity.

Tony and Sikandar, undeterred, stepped into the courtyard, their resolve unshaken. This was the moment they had been working toward, a showdown that would decide the fate of the Obsidian Dawn. Their commitment to justice was unwavering, and their pursuit of the criminal syndicate had led them through countless challenges and near misses.

"Zoya, Rashid," Tony called out, his voice carrying a steely determination. "It's over. Surrender now, and justice will be served."

Zoya, her eyes gleaming with a mixture of defiance and resignation, responded, "You may have tracked us down, but you'll never understand the cause we fight for."

Rashid's voice, equally resolute, echoed her sentiments. "We're not alone in this. The Obsidian Dawn is a force that can't be stopped."

The agents of the Obsidian Dawn shrouded in darkness, remained silent but vigilant. The courtyard was charged with tension, a crucible where opposing ideologies collided in full force. The ancient stones seemed to bear witness to this remarkable faceoff, their timeless presence a testament to the countless struggles that had unfolded within these walls. Tony and Sikandar knew that this confrontation was not just about capturing two operatives. It was about dismantling a notorious entity that had thrived on chaos and disorder. It was a battle between justice and lawlessness, order and anarchy. The agents closed the distance, moving with a precision born of years of training. Their movements were in sync with each other, a hallmark of their association and shared determination. The courtyard, once a place of quiet solitude, had become a battlefield where the clash of wills echoed like a battle cry.

The tension hung in the air like a heavy cloak, the outcome of their mission uncertain. Shadows played tricks on the eye, and every sound was amplified in the stillness of the night. It was a moment where past and present converged, where the weight of history pressed upon the present.

With a sudden, explosive burst of action, the showdown erupted. Shots rang out, and the ancient stones bore witness to a fierce and determined struggle.

The agents of the Obsidian Dawn, operating in the shadows, fought with a tenacity born of desperation. Zoya and Rashid, their cause unwavering, used every ounce of their training to resist capture. Tony and Sikandar, equally determined, moved with an accuracy and discipline that had brought them this far.

With each passing moment, the fate of the Obsidian Dawn hung in the balance. The outcome of this faceoff would determine whether justice would prevail over lawlessness and whether order would conquer chaos. As the agents grappled in the moonlit courtyard, the echoes of their struggle reverberated through the night, an ode to the unwavering commitment of those who fought for what they believed in.

Chapter 10

Unveiling Shadows: The Battle of Minds

After the intense faceoff with Zoya and Rashid, the Obsidian Dawn's once defiant operatives now found themselves locked and chained in a dingy interrogation room.

The intense chase through Istanbul's alleys had led Tony and Sikandar to a run-down courtyard, where Zoya and Rashid had found themselves trapped. As the agents closed in on the operatives, Tony and Sikandar had cut off their escape routes, leaving Zoya and Rashid with no way out. With their guns drawn and adrenaline surging, the operatives had no choice but to surrender.

"Give it up," Tony roared. "There's nowhere to run now."

Once captured, they were handcuffed, their weapons confiscated, and their every move closely monitored. The agents didn't take any chances, ensuring that the operatives couldn't stage a last-minute escape.

With Zoya and Rashid securely in custody, they offered no resistance. They were escorted to be interrogated by Tony and Sikandar, who knew that this was a crucial moment in their pursuit of the Obsidian Dawn, and they were prepared to extract vital information from their captive adversaries.

It was at a secret location located underground in the streets of Istanbul, undetectable and obscure. They were now at the mercy of Tony and Sikandar, who had a different approach to extracting information than most; they would make the operatives an offer that they couldn't refuse. Zoya and Rashid's defiance and ferociousness ceased, and the jig was up. Tony and Sikandar were determined to get whatever information they could, and they would go to the ends of the earth to get it. While seated across from one another in the poorly lit room, Tony's piercing gaze bore into Zoya. Meanwhile, Sikandar focused on Rashid. The air was charged with tension as the agents prepared to extract vital information from their captives.

Tony's voice cut through the silence like a blade, "You know, you can save yourself a world of pain if you cooperate."

Zoya's eyes flickered with defiance, "You can try, but you won't break us."

Sikandar's voice, in contrast, was a low rumble, his words laced with an established authority. "Listen to me, and listen to me carefully. We're here to seek the truth; this doesn't have to be hard. In this room, you choose your own fate."

The interrogation that followed was a battle of wits, a verbal duel that tested the boundaries of strength of character and the facade of deception. Tony and Sikandar were seasoned interrogators and employed their vast knowledge of psychological tactics to probe Zoya and Rashid's vulnerabilities and exploit their fears.

The questions were fired with precision, each word chosen to make the operatives crack under pressure.

"What is the Obsidian Dawn's endgame? Who are your contacts? Where are the other operatives located?" Tony inquired, his voice now getting louder as he grew more frustrated. Zoya and Rashid exchanged guarded glances but remained quiet; their silence spoke volumes, as their loyalty to the Obsidian Dawn remained resolute. It was going to take a lot more for them than to give up their criminal syndicate.

Sikandar leaned forward, his eyes locked onto Rashid. "We know your organization has infiltrated governments and executed international crimes. The world needs to know the culprits behind these acts and put a face to the name of the notorious Obsidian Dawn."

The room had become a battleground of words, every question and response a strategic move in a chess game of information extraction. Tony and Sikandar knew that they needed more than just the capture of Zoya and Rashid to dismantle the Obsidian Dawn and bring the organization's leaders to justice; they needed to unravel the web of intrigue surrounding the syndicate. Hours passed, but the agents remained patient; they hadn't let out a single word that could be used against them or the Obsidian Dawn. Tony and Sikandar, however, wouldn't give up until they had what they were searching for. They would test the operatives' resolve and obtain the information needed to prevent future acts of terrorism. The room was brimming with tension, and the air was heavy with the weight of unspoken secrets and hidden agendas.

As the interrogation continued, the dynamic began to shift, and the operatives' resistance began to fade. Zoya and Rashid, once so elusive and cunning, found themselves trapped in a battle they had not anticipated—the quest for the truth by two agents who were equally unyielding. "Fine. You can stay quiet, but we are not your enemies; should you choose to give up Obsidian Dawn, we'll grant you immunity, a new identity, and a clean slate," Sikandar explained. As the hours stretched on, the firm resolve of Zoya and Rashid began to crumble under the barrage of Tony's questions. Each inquiry was a calculated step towards unraveling the origins and sinister plans of the Obsidian Dawn. Sikandar's acute ability to read their expressions to sense the nuances of their reactions added a razor-sharp edge to the interrogation, leaving no room for deception.

Tony muttered, "Help us understand, and we can bring an end to this."

Worn out by the hours of interrogation, Zoya and Rashid's patience was getting thinner and thinner. Zoya had always been one to watch her own back and jump ship when she thought it was sinking. She thought long and hard about Sikandar's offer of a clean slate, which was too tempting not to avail, given the dire circumstances. The countless hours had made their shoulders slump with defeat.

At that moment, Zoya sang like a canary, laying everything before Tony and Sikandar. "If I tell you this, I want guaranteed protection. For Rashid and I. No charges; a clean slate, like you promised."

Tony and Sikandar looked at each other, a shared expression of affirmation. They looked at Zoya and replied, "You have a deal. Now, talk."

Taking a gulp and a deep breath before speaking, Zoya broke the ice as Rashid gazed at her with his eyes widened, "It started with a belief that the world's systems are flawed. We wanted to expose the hypocrisy of nations." Sikandar leaned in, his voice gentle but firm. "But chaos only breeds more chaos. Your actions endanger innocent lives. How could you not know that before getting into this?" The revelations poured forth—Obsidian Dawn's motivations and misguided ideologies. The operatives's backstories were revealed, and their vulnerabilities were laid bare. The lines between adversaries and individuals blurred, and the intricate layers of their characters came into focus. The revelations provided new perspectives, raising questions about loyalties and hidden agendas.

Zoya spoke first, her voice carrying a hint of remorse, "We believed that by shaking the foundations of the world's power structures, we could expose the truth. We thought we were fighting for justice."

Rashid, still defiant in his tone that had a trace of uncertainty, added, "The Obsidian Dawn grew out of a desire to disrupt the corrupt systems that oppress the vulnerable. We never intended for innocent lives to be caught in the crossfire."

Tony and Sikandar exchanged glances as they studied the flawed motives of the syndicate from the eyes of two operatives who had been led astray. The story of the Obsidian Dawn was no longer a simple tale of good versus evil; there was something much more complex simmering under the surface.

These people, like many others ensnared by the syndicate, were driven by a misguided sense of justice, and their revelations humanized them, revealing the scars of past injustices that had fueled their actions. Sikandar leaned back, his gaze never leaving Rashid. "It's time to make amends, to help us dismantle the Obsidian Dawn and prevent further harm. But I'll ask you this: Why? Why did you do it? Even when you knew you were being used as mere pawns?" The room fell into deafening silence as Zoya and Rashid grappled with the choices before them. The boundaries of their loyalties had shifted, and their resolve had been shaken. The revelations had added layers to the conflict, shedding light on the human elements behind the Obsidian Dawn's actions.

"We had no choice. Or, so we thought," Rashid added. "We were young, impressionable, and looking for a cause to fight for. They told us we would be heroes. "

"What's their next move? First, it was releasing the poisonous gas into the Palace; now, what'll it be, bombing the White House?" Tony asked.

"We don't know. They've left Istanbul, and we lost all connection with them when we left the Palace," replied Zoya.

As Tony and Sikandar ended the interrogation, they knew that the path ahead would be fraught with uncertainty. The agents were determined to use this knowledge to bring the Obsidian Dawn to its knees while offering a chance at redemption for those who had once been their foes. As the puzzle pieces fell into place, Tony and Sikandar delved deeper into Obsidian Dawn's intricate plans to calculate their next move. Their investigation would soon lead them deeper into a maze of secrets, where allies and enemies were not always distinguishable.

"We're going to keep you here for a while. When it's safe, we'll let you go," Sikandar said as he and Tony left the room after untying Rashid and Zoya.

***

In a safe house in another discreet location, Tony and Sikandar concentrated on the documents and decrypted files that they had come across while investigating the Obsidian Dawn and its origins. They slowly began to connect the dots that painted a larger picture. Conversations with informants and allies shed light on the obsidian dawn's origins—an underground movement born from disillusionment and discontent.

Sikandar's eyes squinted as he keenly studied a decrypted message found in his investigation and shared his findings with Tony. "The Obsidian Dawn has attracted people from various walks of life—idealists, hackers, and mercenaries. They're all bound by a common goal – chaos and dismantling the status quo."

Tony, whose fingers were tracing a timeline on a map, nodded in agreement. "Their goal was to collapse the systems they thought as corrupting the world, to expose the hypocrisy that runs deep within governments and institutions. Their goal isn't flawed; it's their means to get there."

The revelations unraveled a narrative of disillusionment, where individuals from diverse backgrounds had found themselves drawn to the cause of the Obsidian Dawn. These were not mere criminals; they were people driven by an impenetrable sense of injustice who believed that their actions were a means to an end—a way to bring about the change they desperately sought.

As the agents focused on analyzing documents and decrypting messages, they managed to piece together Obsidian Dawn's origins. It had emerged as a syndicate that had offered seekers of justice a way to channel their frustration into something that would impact global foreign politics and grab the attention of world leaders to get their message across. The motives of the Obsidian Dawn added a new layer of depth to the scenario. "It's a flawed ideology," Sikandar pondered as frustration overpowered him. "They sought to change the world for the better, but their methods are causing chaos in the world, with innocents being collateral damage."

Tony's gaze remained fixed on the map as he contemplated the situation. "We need to address the root causes but also put an end to the havoc they've wreaked."

Their mission, which had started as a pursuit to apprehend criminals and prevent an impending catastrophe, had transformed into a confusing maze of moral ambiguity. Tony and Sikandar found themselves navigating a treacherous path where loyalties were no longer clear-cut, and the lines between right and wrong began to blur.

One thing, however, was clear: the revelation of Obsidian Dawn's history and formation had given rise to empathy. Rashid and Zoya, like countless others, were mere victims of a system they perceived as corrupt, and their actions were, in their minds, at least, a desperate cry for justice.

Tony and Sikandar now felt a growing sense of urgency with each passing minute. They were not just agents on a mission to apprehend criminals; they were now tasked with figuring out Obsidian Dawn's next move in order to protect the world from their chaos. It was a quest for justice, and the clock was ticking. Their operation would require them to not only disintegrate the criminal syndicate but to uncover the deep-seated issues that had given rise to it. As the investigation took a suspicious turn, they followed a trail of breadcrumbs that led to long-buried secrets that would turn the investigation on its head. Their chase of Obsidian Dawn took them to a point in history that struck a deeply personal chord, a revelation that threatened to shatter their understanding of the mission. The two agents put together the missing pieces of the puzzle and were shocked by what they stumbled upon.

Sikandar, whose tone was but a faint whisper, said, "The Obsidian Dawn's origins trace back to a series of events years ago—an event that *we* were complicit in."

Tony's eyes widened in disbelief. "What do you mean?"

"Take a look; it's all right here," replied Sikandar.

"It can't be... this... this is what changed everything for us," Tony's voice now in high pitch.

"Everything we thought we knew..." Sikandar's voice trailed off, the gravity of the situation sinking in.

Tony's thoughts raced, memories resurfacing in a new light. "Our choices back then, they rippled through time and became the catalyst for this."

Years ago, a faction of the RAW agents was involved in a high-stakes incident that had far-reaching consequences. This event had been a catalyst, altering the course of their lives and ultimately leading them to their roles as RAW agents in the first place. Their actions then had unknowingly played a role in creating the conditions that prompted the formation of the Obsidian Dawn. While they were not directly responsible for its creation, the repercussions of the event they were involved in had a cascading effect. Their pro-government actions prompted the people who would later become part of the Obsidian Dawn. The criminal syndicate was born out of a desire to challenge and dismantle the systems they perceived as corrupt. Obsidian Dawn's motivations, therefore, were not only born from their actions but were influenced by the environment and conditions created in the aftermath of the event in which Tony and Sikandar played a role.

The revelation of this connection cast a shadow over the agents' mission as they realized that their past actions had inadvertently fueled the fire that was now raging in the form of Obsidian Dawn. It became a quest for redemption and an opportunity to correct the consequences of their actions from the past. The agents not only had to bring the criminal organization to justice but also navigated the intricacies of their own past choices and their impact on the world they had sworn to protect.

With a newfound understanding of the interconnectedness of their fates, the agents now prepared to confront the Obsidian Dawn's leaders. The revelation raised questions about the blurred lines between good and evil, hero and villain. They were no longer dealing with a faceless enemy but confronting a reflection of themselves in the Obsidian Dawn, which was a manifestation of the consequences of their actions, a living reminder of the intricate interplay between choices made in the past and the impact they had on the present. Their mission was an opportunity to bring closure to a chapter they had thought was long behind them. Tony's fingers traced the rim of his coffee cup as he spoke softly, the weariness evident in his voice. "It's hard to ignore that our actions might have unintentionally fueled this fire."

Sikandar's eyes were lost in a distant memory, the lines on his forehead creasing with each thought. "But we've walked a long path since then. The lives we've saved, all the good we've done—it's gotta count for something."

Aisha, who had entered the room quietly, offered a comforting notion. "We're not defined by our past; our actions of today now matter just as much."

Chapter 11

Fractured Loyalties: Navigating Shadows of Doubt

Sitting in the in safehouse, which had became a haven for shadows and secrets, the revelation of the agent's shared history with the Obsidian Dawn began to cast long shadows over their mission. Tony and Sikander had always prided themselves of a clear sense of purpose they derived from working as undercover agents. But, now they found themselves thrust into a world of moral ambiguity and doubt.

The intricate web of connections, the weight of their past choices, and the consequences of those very choices were challenged their long-held and staunch beliefs. As the realization of their past actions of fueling the fire that was now the Obsidian Dawn took hold, the once-unbreakable walls of their certainty began to crumble. In the midst of their personal conflicts, the mission itself began to transform. It was no longer just about stopping a criminal syndicate; it had become a journey of self-discovery, a quest for redemption, and a mission to address the root causes of the Obsidian Dawn's existence.

The revelation of their interconnected fates left Tony and Sikandar questioning the very essence of their mission; which they had made their life's purpose. They had always believed themselves to be on the side of justice, but now, they began to question their loyalties.

As doubt engulfed them, Aisha tried to be a source of comfort in this time. Her voice cut through the uncertainty that had taken root, "Look, I can't speak to the intentions of the Obsidian Dawn, but I know one thing: we can't let the past hinder our future. Mistakes get made, and people get hurt. That's just..the way it is. We have to come to terms with that."

Beneath the surface of their façade, the revelation of their shared history with the Obsidian Dawn had stirred personal conflicts within Tony and Sikandar. As they navigated the treacherous terrain of international espionage, the complexities of their past choices and their connection reared its ugly head, and now their mission was compromised with personal convictions. Now, it was a whirlwind of emotions and dilemmas that tested the very core of their identities.

Tony, the embodiment of determination, found himself grappling with an inner turmoil that he had rarely experienced before. With his voice tinged with vulnerability, he lamented, "I just…don't know where I belong anymore. This is all I knew…was it all a lie?" his gaze met Sikander's, who understood the look of his despair.

He had always been led to believe in the clear-cut differentiation between right and wrong, a black-and-white world where agents fought against the forces of darkness, like the Obisdian Dawn. But now, the revelation of their past actions indirectly contributing to the formation of the Obsidian Dawn had blurred those lines.

The mission they had undertaken was no longer just about apprehending criminals; it was about confronting the consequences of their own actions. The weight of their shared history bore down on him making every decision feel like a moral dilemma. Tony continued, "I used to see the world in absolutes, black and white, right and wrong. But now…it's all shades of gray. I wonder, were our actions really justified, if it led to the formation and thriving of the Obsidian Dawn?"

Sikandar, who was equally distraught, had always exuded quiet strength and steadfast resolve, but also found himself being plagued by arising personal conflicts. The memories of a time long gone, the choices they had made, and the realization that they had played an unintentional role in the Obsidian Dawn's emergence, haunted his thoughts. The lives they had saved and the good they had done since that event offered some solace, but they were merely moments of consolation.

Sikandar nodded in understanding, and said, "Looks like our past has finally caught up with us… and it's forcing us to confront the consequences of our actions. Think about the lives we've saved since then... they matter, but can they ever truly outweigh the unintended harm we've indirectly contributed to?"

"This revelation…it's clouded my ability to see the way forward anymore. The mission feels different, and the lines between right and wrong are so…*blurred*."

Sikandar replied, "We're not just intelligence agents; we're seekers of redemption."

Aisha, the anchor in their turbulent journey, interjected, "We can't change the past, but we can shape the future.. We have to find a way to make amends and ensure that the world is better for our presence."

The atmosphere was heavy with uncertainty, as the room fell silent. Tony, Sikandar, and Aisha sat around a table, the soft glow of monitors casting eerie shadows on their faces. The revelation of their shared history with the criminal syndicate had shaken their convictions, but it had also forged an unbreakable bond between them. They sought answers to the questions that weighed on their hearts, and found solace in their shared burden of decisions, recognizing that they could navigate the complexities of their past and find a path to redemption.

"Makes you think," Sikandar croaked. "That actions of the past have such an influence on our identity."

Aisha took note of the emotional whirlwind that raged within Tony and Sikandar. She recognized that their past was a specter that clung to their every move, complicating the already complex world of intelligence and espionage. She was their anchor, a voice of reason in the tumultuous sea of emotions, a reminder that they were not defined by their past actions but by their present choices. All of them now viewed Obsidian Dawn's peratives as more than just adversaries but as individuals driven by their convictions and experiences, which conflicted with their mission.

Their conversations delved into the depths of their contemplation. Tony and Sikandar questioned the very essence of their mission and recognized that the operatives they chased were not just anonymous rivals, but people with their own stories and motivations.

Aisha's voice rang out with reassurance,"The idea that actions and history shape identity isn't just a theoretical concept anymore. It's our reality, and something we have to confront. Zoya and Rashid…they must have their own stories, their own reasons." Each step in the mission was now a tightrope walk between the conflicting principles of justice and redemption. The faces of the Obsidian Dawn's operatives, who were once enemies, were now a reflection of their own past. This transformation turned every confrontation into a personal battle, where the agents had to grapple not only with the mission's objectives but also with their own internal conflicts. In the face of uncertainty, they pondered the very nature of heroism and justice.

Tony asked, "Can we still call ourselves *heroes* when our past choices have contributed to the existence of the Obsidian Dawn? Given all the harm they've caused in the world."

Sikandar, finding strength in his commitment to the future, declared, "Our mission…is now a quest for redemption, a chance to make amends. We can't change the past, but we can shape the future."

Their pursuit of justice was fueled by their shared sense of purpose and a desire to confront their emerging doubts. They had come to terms with the idea that actions and history shaped identity in profound ways, and that their journey was not just a matter of intelligence and espionage but a personal pursuit for redemption.

Aisha continued to offer words of reassurance, "The complexities of our choices have challenged our beliefs, but they've also shown us the importance of growth and change. Obsidian Dawn chose an evil path, and that's on their conscious. We do the best we can, to save as many as we can. Their end goal isn't entirely wrong; it's the means."

"You're right. We will stand for what we've always stood for: justice," Tony's voice laden with confidence and resolve.

"This mission has challenged everything I thought I knew. But maybe I needed to renew my perspective," Sikandar added. "We can agree with the goals of the Obsidian Dawn, but they're wreaking havoc on the world, blinded by their pursuit."

The whirlwind of emotions and dilemmas they faced ultimately strengthened their resolve. They began to understand that their mission was not merely a matter of apprehending criminals and preventing an impending catastrophe; it was a journey to confront the shadows of their own past. It was a mission that required them to differentiate the complexities of morality and personal conflict while striving to protect the world from the consequences of their actions. In this whirlwind of personal conflicts and moral dilemmas, the agents found themselves redefining their roles as intelligence agents. They had to balance the scales of their own past actions and ensure a better future for the world they had sworn to protect.

As the days turned into weeks and the missions piled up, the trio found solace in their renewed perspectives. They understood that their journey was far from over, and that they needed to confront their past and seek a path to redemption.They knew that their past would forever be a part of who they were, but they also believed in the power of their present choices to shape a brighter future. Navigating the shadows of doubt, they continued their relentless pursuit of justice, determined to make amends for their shared history with the Obsidian Dawn.

"One thing I know for sure: we need to protect the world from the consequences of their actions, and take down the Obsidian Dawn," Aisha said, her tone firm. "With each life we save, we make amends for the past. Because each life is precious."

The reassurance of their shared purpose began to cast a warm light in the midst of the darkness that threatened to engulf them.

"We can't erase our past, but we could navigate the present and the future with a renewed commitment to justice," Tony roared.

Tony and Sikandar shared burden of decisions that were made long in the past, with a newfound resolve to continue striving for a better future. They had always believed in the power of their choices to make a difference, and this belief was a lifeline in the sea of doubt that had suddenly engulfed them. The revelation of their intertwined fates was a turning point in their mission.

With Aisha's words serving as a guiding light in the midst of the darkness, their mission had taken on an even deeper meaning, for it wasn't just about capturing the Obsidian Dawn' operatives anymore. It was about addressing the root causes of its existence, and what led it to pursue the means that they did. It was a chance to rectify the consequences of their past actions.

The road ahead was uncertain, but the understanding that their actions now mattered just as much gave them the strength to face the challenges that lay ahead.

The agents were no longer defined solely by their past choices; they were defined by the choices they made in the present. The revelation of their shared history had cast shadows and doubts, but it had also illuminated a path towards a future where heroes confronted the shadows of their past and sought to make a positive difference. The room, once heavy with the weight of revelation, now held a sense of shared purpose. Tony and Sikandar had faced the demons of their past, and while the road ahead was uncertain, their mission to protect the world from chaos remained unshaken. The journey ahead was a tangle of uncertainties, but it was one they were adamant to tread, clutching on to the belief that their actions could still make a difference in the chaotic and divided world.

Chapter 12

Shadow's Covert Counterstrike

As Tony and Sikandar delved deeper into their investigation, doubts began to cloud their minds. Zoya and Rashid's interrogation had yielded unsettling inconsistencies that gnawed at the edges of their certainty.

Alibis crumbled under scrutiny, timelines tangled in contradiction, and vital details remained conspicuously absent. Despite their best efforts to extract the truth, Zoya and Rashid's evasive demeanor only fueled the agents' suspicions further. Tony and Sikandar couldn't shake the feeling that something wasn't adding up. The tension in the interrogation room hung heavy as they grappled with the unsettling realization that their suspects might be hiding more than they were letting on.

Determined, the agents resolved to press on, adamant to uncover the secrets lurking beneath the surface. Little did they know, their pursuit of the truth would lead them down a labyrinth of deception and danger, where the line between ally and adversary blurred with each passing revelation.

Up until this point, Rashid and Zoya had endured relentless questioning and torture at the hands of Tony and Sikandar. The agents were determined to extract the truth from the operatives of the Obsidian Dawn, but Rashid and Zoya remained steadfast in their silence. As the interrogation continued, the agents had gotten an incoming call from the head of R&AW, Yuvraj Singhania. With a mixture of anticipation and apprehension, Tony, Sikandar, and Aisha glanced at each other when Rashid broke out into maniacal laughter; his smug expression betrayed a hint of confidence. "Go on, pick up the call," Rashid taunted them, his voice laced with arrogance. "I'm pretty sure they would have gotten the video of the Indian dignitaries being caught by now. We always had plan B in case things went south. And we knew you guys were here in Istanbul."

With a deep breath, Aisha accepted the call, and the screen flickered to life, revealing the stern visage of Yuvraj Singhania.

"Agent Aisha, report," Yuvraj commanded, his tone unwavering.

Aisha cleared her throat, her voice betraying a hint of uncertainty as she replied, "Sir, we have successfully apprehended the operatives of the Obsidian Dawn, Zoya and Rashid. However, they have been uncooperative during interrogation."

As Aisha spoke, Tony and Sikandar stood behind her, their eyes fixed on the screen. On the video conference feed, the grim reality of the situation unfolded as footage of the captured Indian dignitaries, bound and gagged, with bombs strapped to their bodies, played out before their eyes.

Yuvraj's expression darkened as he surveyed the scene, his voice grave. "This is a dire situation. We cannot allow harm to come to our dignitaries. We must act swiftly to secure their release."

In the interrogation room, Rashid's laughter echoed, a stark contrast to the gravity of the situation unfolding before them. Tony's jaw clenched with frustration, his gaze burning with determination.

"We thought it was the end when we caught them," Tony began, his voice tinged with regret. "But the story is far from over."

With a heavy heart, Sikandar added, "We must find a way to resolve this before it's too late."

Yuvraj Singhania's voice cut through the tension, his tone resolute. "Agent Tony, Agent Sikandar, I trust you to handle this situation with the utmost care and urgency. The lives of our dignitaries depend on it."

As the video conference ended, Tony and Sikandar exchanged a silent nod, and their resolve hardened. Rashid's laughter faded into the background as they turned their attention back to the interrogation room, where Zoya and Rashid awaited their fate. With time running out and the stakes higher than ever, Tony and Sikandar knew that they would need to make difficult decisions to ensure the safety of the captured dignitaries and bring an end to the reign of the Obsidian Dawn once and for all.

"Let's make a deal, Tony," Rashid's voice sliced through the room. "I'll release the Indian dignitaries, but in return, you and your team have to take their place and set us free. And... you have to release someone– Malik Al-Hassan."

"Malik Al-Hassan?" gasped Tony.

"Are you out of your mind?" Sikandar growled. "We can't release him; he's a threat and menace to society!"

Rashid leaned forward, his voice firm, "Not only will you relieve him, but Malik Al Hassan will be allowed to leave the country - *unharmed.* No interference from law enforcement or intelligence agencies. He should have safe passage, and state-of-the-art- technological arms should be sent with him. Do we have a deal?"

Tony and Sikandar hesitated, weighing Rashid's proposal. "And what of the technological advancements you seek?"

Rashid's gaze remained steady. "We need the best India has to offer to ensure Malik's safe passage. I give you 30 minutes to decide and respond."

Tension hung heavy in the air; Zoya glanced at Rashid, concern etched on her face. "Do you think they'll agree?"

Rashid shrugged, his expression unreadable. "Time will tell."

"You've got thirty minutes to think it over. Make the right choice."

As Rashid's proposal hung in the air, the tension in the interrogation room reached a palpable crescendo. Tony's jaw tightened, his eyes flashing with a mixture of anger and frustration. Sikandar's expression mirrored Tony's, his fists clenched in silent rage. Aisha, the voice of reason amidst the turmoil, exchanged a glance with her teammates, her expression reflecting a deep sense of unease.

"You'll release the Indian dignitaries?" Her voice was laced with incredulity. "And what guarantee do we have that you'll uphold your end of the bargain, Rashid?"

Rashid's smirk widened, a cunning gleam in his eyes. "You have my word, Tony. We may be adversaries, but even we have our codes of honor. I assure you, the dignitaries will be released unharmed."

"What about us? You expect us to simply trust you and walk into captivity?" Sikandar's voice was edged with skepticism.

Rashid's gaze flickered between Tony and Sikandar, his expression unreadable. "It's a risk you'll have to take."

Tony, Sikandar, and Aisha went over to the other room to discuss their next steps away from the prying eyes and ears of the operatives. The atmosphere in the room was heavy with resignation as Tony, Sikandar, and Aisha faced the harsh reality of their situation. Options dwindled, and uncertainty loomed over their next move. The weight of their decision to accept Rashid's deal hung heavily on their shoulders, but with the lives of the Indian dignitaries at stake, they saw no other choice.

Tony's frustration boiled over, his hand slamming against the wall with a resounding thud. "We don't have time for this! Lives are at stake here!"

"We need to think this through carefully. Rashid's proposal may be our only chance to secure the release of the dignitaries." Aisha stepped forward, her voice calm but firm.

Tony shot Aisha a pointed look; his frustration was evident. "And what about our safety, Aisha? Are we willing to sacrifice ourselves for the sake of others?"

Aisha's gaze softened, her resolve unwavering. "We've faced tough choices before, Tony. Sometimes sacrifices are necessary to achieve a greater good."

Sikandar's voice cut through the tension, his tone measured. "We don't have much time. We need to make a decision."

"We're running out of time," Tony muttered, his voice strained with frustration. "We have to accept Rashid's deal, even if it means putting ourselves in danger."

After a tense discussion among them, Tony, Sikandar, and Aisha found themselves with little choice but to accept Rashid's deal, unsure of what the future held. With heavy hearts and apprehension gnawing at their resolve, they made their way to the room where Zoya and Rashid awaited to finalize the agreement.

Zoya's gaze held a glimmer of defiance, while Rashid's smirk betrayed a hint of satisfaction. Tony squared his shoulders, his gaze unwavering as he addressed them.

Before Sikandar stepped into the room, he discreetly retrieved a small microchip – a GPS tracker – from his pocket. With swift precision, he connected the chip to his phone and concealed it within his shoe. With a sense of urgency, Sikandar sent the location of their whereabouts to R&AW headquarters, along with a brief message detailing the gravity of the situation.

Once the message was sent, Sikandar swiftly deleted any trace of the communication from his phone before returning it to his pocket. As he entered the room where Zoya and Rashid were bound, tension hung thick in the air.

Rashid's smirk widened into a sinister grin, his eyes gleaming with mischief. "You have my word, Tony. We're men of honor, after all."

With a sense of unease settling in the pit of his stomach, Tony exchanged a wary glance with his teammates. The die was cast, and now all they could do was wait for the inevitable to unfold.

As Zoya and Rashid were untied, Tony, Sikandar, and Aisha exchanged worried looks, their senses on high alert. The sudden turn of events had caught them off guard, and they braced themselves for whatever Rashid had planned next. He wasted no time in requesting their weapons and mobile devices, a request met with cautious compliance from the agents.

Tony hesitated for a moment, his hand lingering on the holster at his side, before reluctantly complying. As they relinquished their weapons and phones, a sense of vulnerability washed over them, their instincts screaming a warning.

Rashid seized this opportunity to make a call to his accomplices, instructing them to converge on their location. With a heavy heart, Tony and his team exchanged glances, silently steeling themselves for what was to come.

Rashid's men arrived in two ominous black jeeps, their figures obscured by full black attire and masks. The sight sent a chill down Tony's spine, a sinking feeling settling in the pit of his stomach. In a swift turn of events, the roles were reversed as Zoya and Rashid's team arrived.

Before they knew it, Tony, Sikandar, and Aisha found themselves handcuffed and blindfolded, their captors showing no mercy as they were ushered into the waiting vehicles. The drive felt endless, each passing moment filled with a sense of dread and uncertainty. Now, at the mercy of their foes, Tony couldn't help but wonder if they had made the right decision. Only time would tell if their gamble would pay off or if they had fallen victim to Rashid's cunning once again. Finally, after what seemed like an eternity, the vehicles came to a stop at a desolate warehouse. As they were led inside and the blindfolds were removed, Tony's eyes slowly adjusted to the dimly lit surroundings. His heart sank as he took in the sight of the Indian dignitaries, bound and gagged, seated nearby.

Sikandar's voice broke the tense silence, his words tinged with resignation, "You have us now, so let them leave."

"You think we would miss such a wonderful opportunity?" Zoya's laughter cut through the air like a knife, her tone mocking.

Tony's mind raced, searching for a way out of their dire predicament. But before he could formulate a plan,

Rashid moved to his setup, his fingers flying across the keyboard with practiced ease. With a click of a button, a video call was initiated, the encrypted network ensuring their conversation remained private.

As the head of R&AW appeared on the screen, Rashid wasted no time in laying out his demands. Tony watched helplessly as Rashid presented his leverage—the captured Indian dignitaries—before outlining his terms for their release.

While the conversation between Rashid and Yuvraj unfolded, Tony's mind raced with possibilities. They were trapped, with no means of escape, and Rashid held all the cards. But as the conversation reached its climax, Tony's gaze flickered to Sikandar, a silent understanding passing between them. With a subtle nod, Sikandar signaled to Tony, his eyes glinting with determination. Despite the odds stacked against them, they refused to give up hope. Together, they would find a way to turn the tide and emerge victorious, no matter the cost. As Yuvraj Singhania scrambled to address Rashid's urgent demand, tension hung thick in the air. Time was ticking away, each passing second bringing them closer to a grim deadline. With the lives of the Indian dignitaries and their agents hanging in the balance, the pressure mounted with each passing moment.

Yuvraj's voice crackled over the communications link as he relayed the gravity of the situation to his superiors, his words weighted with urgency, "We need a decision, and we need it now. Rashid has given us one hour, or else..."

As the seconds ticked by, a sense of foreboding settled over the room, the weight of the impending disaster bearing down on everyone present. Suddenly, the atmosphere erupted into chaos as blood spilled from the head of one of Rashid's men, followed by four more in rapid succession. Panic gripped the room as the reality of their perilous situation dawned on them.

In the midst of the chaos, Sikandar's sharp instincts kicked in, his eyes scanning the room for a means of escape. With a whispered instruction to Tony, he gestured for them to raise their hands above their heads. In a stroke of luck or perhaps fate, their handcuffs shattered into pieces, freeing them from their restraints.

Without hesitation, Tony and Sikandar sprang into action, rolling towards the fallen bodies of Rashid's men. With deft movements, they seized the fallen men's weapons, their training kicking in as they unleashed a barrage of gunfire against their assailants. Amidst the chaos of the firefight, a shadowy figure emerged, his presence like a specter in the night. He moved with stealth and precision, his sniper rifle picking off Rashid's men with deadly accuracy. His identity was shrouded in mystery, his actions swift and decisive.

As the dust settled and the last of Rashid's men fell, the mysterious figure melted into the shadows, disappearing as quickly as he had appeared. His nickname, "Shadow," whispered among the survivors as a testament to his elusive nature.

In the aftermath of the firefight, as the dust settled and the smoke cleared, Sikandar found a moment to express his gratitude to Yuvraj Singhania, the head of R&AW.

"Thanks for Shadow," he said, his voice filled with appreciation for the unknown ally who had turned the tide in their favor.

Yuvraj nodded solemnly, his expression reflecting a mix of relief and appreciation.

"We owe him a debt of gratitude," he replied, his voice tinged with reverence for the mysterious figure who had saved their lives. But, when Shadow made his move and chaos erupted, Rashid's deal with R&AW seemed to crumble.

"The deal is off," he muttered under his breath, frustration evident in his voice. Zoya's eyes widened in alarm. "What do we do now?"

Rashid's mind raced as he assessed the situation. "We adapt," he replied, determination flashing in his eyes. As the dust settled, it became clear that Rashid's plan had backfired, leaving them in a precarious position.

Chapter 13

Tangled Paths

In the aftermath of the intense showdown, the Indian dignitaries were still being held captive, as the deal was now off. Tony and Sikandar, the two lead operatives of R&AW, ensured that every precaution was taken to free them. Armored vehicles escorted the convoy, sharpshooters scanned the horizon for any sign of trouble, and a special air force contingent patrolled the skies. Their mission, a tense, high-stakes operation, had culminated in failure.

Now, another wrinkle remained in their otherwise immaculate plan: Zoya and Rashid, the operatives of Obsidian Dawn. After a humiliating defeat at the hands of R&AW, their carefully orchestrated scheme lay in shambles, along with the deal they had made.

Despite the gravity of their past actions, Tony and Sikandar had made a bold decision. Under constant supervision and heavy surveillance, Zoya and Rashid would be brought back to India to R&AW Headquarters in New Delhi, India, along with their team.

"I don't know if it's a good idea to bring them back with us," Aisha said, her brow furrowed with worry as she voiced her reservations.

Tony placed a reassuring hand on her shoulder, his expression serious and determined.

"We need to find out more about the Obsidian Dawn and their plans. Zoya and Rashid might hold valuable information that could help us. Besides, we can't let them go now, not after the stunts they've pulled. It'll give us some leverage on Obsidian Dawn, too."

"We'll keep a close watch on them. They won't be able to cause any trouble under our watch," Sikandar nodded in agreement, his eyes reflecting the weight of their decision.

After a meticulous overview, they chartered planes to fly Zoya, Rashid, and their crew back to India. The atmosphere during the flight was tense, a microcosm of the larger situation. Usually arrogant, Zoya and Rashid sat stiffly in their seats, nervously glancing at the watchful R&AW agents. The plane's engines droned on, a constant hum that seemed to amplify every little sound - a cough, a rustle of clothes - in the cramped space. Security guards kept a close eye on them, their hands hovering near their guns, a reminder of the gravity of the situation.

With their poised assurance, Tony and Sikandar stood on either side of the apprehended operatives. Their friendship, developed over innumerable operations, sharply contrasted with the chaos that characterized Zoya and Rashid's squad. The formerly orderly team of agents now bore the look of a group of lost souls, their faces marked with a mix of uncertainty and fear.

As far as Zoya and Rashid were concerned, their world was crumbling. Everything they had built was gone, replaced by the emptiness of defeat. They exchanged quick glances, silently questioning their future. Was this the end? Or was there a sliver of hope to turn things around?

Aware of the tension, the flight attendants tiptoed around, their forced smiles failing to mask the awkwardness. Even the plane's usual humdrum seemed charged with anticipation. This wasn't just a flight back to India but a journey into the unknown, the start of perhaps another high-stakes game. Rashid broke the silence first, his tone filled with a mixture of defiance and resignation.

"You think you can trust us after everything?"

Sikandar's gaze was steady as he responded, his voice firm.

"We don't have much of a choice. But make no mistake, we'll be watching your every move."

Zoya remained silent, her thoughts a mystery to the rest of the team. Tony studied her carefully, noting the flicker of uncertainty in her eyes.

"Any sudden moves and you'll regret it," Tony warned, his tone leaving no room for negotiation.

The flight stretched on for what seemed like an eternity, tension simmering beneath the surface until the team returned to Indian territory. As soon as the chartered planes touched down in New Delhi, the tension that had simmered throughout the flight reached a boiling point. After a tense journey back to India, Zoya and Rashid found themselves enveloped in darkness, their faces covered with black cloths upon landing. The unfamiliar sensation added to their mounting apprehension as they were guided into waiting vehicles, emanating an aura of mystery and secrecy.

Disoriented and disarmed, they were then ushered into the vehicles, the worn leather seats cool against their skin. The rhythmic thrum of the engine was the only sound that dared to intrude on the tense silence. Through the tinted windows, the vibrant chaos of New Delhi blurred by, a stark contrast to the chilling certainty that their destination was a place hidden from even the most discerning eyes. Only the RAW agents knew where they were headed, and even less was known about precisely why they were being taken there.

The message, however, was clear: they were prisoners, their movements controlled, and their fate uncertain. The once-powerful operatives of the Obsidian Dawn were now just passengers on a journey into the unknown.

"Hey! What's the meaning of this?!" Rashid snarled, his voice muffled by the cloth.

A firm hand gripped his arm.

"Silence," Tony's low voice commanded.

Amid the chaos, Zoya remained noticeably quiet, but her body tensed under the sudden restraint.

Inside, the air crackled with a mix of fear and defiance. The journey seemed to stretch on forever until the vehicles finally came to a halt. The engines switched off, leaving an unsettling silence in their wake. Zoya's heart raced with uncertainty as she felt the vehicle lurch into motion, the rhythmic hum of the engine serving as a constant reminder of their precarious situation.

"Where are you taking us?" Rashid stammered, his voice barely a whisper.

No answer came from the R&AW agents, their faces obscured in the shadows of the van. Upon arrival, Zoya and Rashid were escorted to a secure facility for further questioning and debriefing. One by one, they were helped out of the vehicles, still blinded by the black cloths. They stumbled onto solid ground, the sound of gravel crunching under their feet. "Alright, out," Sikandar and Tony ordered, manhandling Zoya and Rashid.

The tension in the air was palpable as they sat in a dimly lit room, their hands bound tightly behind the chairs. Zoya's pulse quickened the moment the black cloth was removed from her face, revealing the stark reality of their surroundings.

As the fabric fell away, revealing the setting in which they found themselves, Rashid and Zoya exchanged a nervous glance. The room barely illuminated the shadowy figures looming in the corners. Their hearts pounded in their chests as they awaited the next twist in their fate. Slowly, as their eyes adjusted to the dim light, they began to make out the shapes of the individual seated beside them.

The realization sent shockwaves through their bodies, their minds reeling with a whirlwind of emotions. Fear, uncertainty, and a flicker of hope battled for dominance as they struggled to come to terms with this unexpected turn of events.

Their captors remained silent, their expressions unreadable as they observed Rashid and Zoya's reactions. At that moment, the air was thick with tension as the weight of the unknown hung heavily on their senses.

Rashid's mind raced, his breath caught in his throat as he tried to make sense of the situation. Meanwhile, Zoya's thoughts whirled with questions: how did this person seated next to them end up in a similar situation?

Rashid's eyes widened in shock as he took in the unexpected sight before him.

"Malik Al-Hassan," Zoya murmured, her voice tinged with disbelief.

Rashid's voice trembled as he addressed Malik, his words laced with a mixture of apprehension and resignation.

The atmosphere inside the room was thick with tension as Rashid and Zoya found themselves seated next to Malik Al Hassan. Each breath felt heavy, the weight of their predicament pressing down on them like a suffocating blanket. Rashid could feel the tension radiating from Malik, mirroring his own unease.

Malik Al Hassan remained silent, his expression inscrutable as he regarded them with a steely gaze. Rashid and Zoya exchanged a glance, their hopes for answers dwindling with each passing moment.

Zoya and Rashid sat in silence, their faces drawn with tension and anxiety. The air in the room felt heavy, suffused with the weight of the consequences of their actions. Malik Al Hassan's furious gaze bore down on them, his anger palpable as he paced back and forth in front of them.

"You two have some nerve," Malik seethed, his voice laced with venom. "I trusted you to uphold your end of the deal, and you betrayed me."

Zoya swallowed hard, her throat dry with shame. "We... we didn't mean for things to go this way, Malik. It was out of our hands."

Rashid nodded in agreement, his expression pained. "We had no control over what happened. The situation escalated beyond our expectations."

Malik's eyes narrowed, his frustration boiling over. "Excuses won't save you now. You've made enemies out of me, and I don't take kindly to betrayal."

As the gravity of their predicament sank in, Zoya and Rashid exchanged a worried glance. They knew they were in deep trouble, and there was no easy way out of the mess they had created.

"We're sorry, Malik," Zoya murmured, her voice barely above a whisper. "We never intended for things to turn out like this; we thought our plan was foolproof."

But Malik was unforgiving, his anger unyielding. "Sorry won't cut it. You've jeopardized everything I've worked for, and sooner or later, you'll pay the price."

Malik's menacing presence loomed over them like a dark cloud; they were pressed for time, and the circumstances were far from being in their favor. Zoya felt a surge of fear grip her heart as she cast a desperate glance at Rashid, silently pleading for a way out of their dire situation. But Rashid could offer no solace, his own fear mirroring hers. They were both trapped in a nightmare of their own making, with no hope of escape.

At that moment, as the weight of their failure hung heavy in the air, Zoya and Rashid could only hope that they would come up with a way to make amends for what they had done. But for now, all they could do was face the consequences of their actions and pray for a chance at redemption.

Chapter 14

Failed Bargain

Malik Al-Hassan was once a prominent underworld figure known for his cunning and ruthlessness. Born into a life of poverty and hardship, he turned to a life of crime at a young age, seeking power and wealth by any means necessary.

His wrongdoings began with petty thefts and street fights, but his ambitions soared to greater heights as he grew older. Malik Al-Hassan soon became involved in more serious crimes, including extortion, smuggling, and drug trafficking. He built a vast criminal empire, ruling through fear and intimidation, with a network of loyal followers at his command.

Despite his success, Malik Al-Hassan's reign of terror did not go unnoticed by the authorities. R&AW had been closely monitoring his activities for years, gathering evidence of his illegal dealings and human rights abuses.

One of the main reasons Malik Al-Hassan was arrested by R&AW was his involvement in a series of terrorist attacks targeting innocent civilians. He orchestrated bombings and assassinations, spreading chaos and fear throughout the region. R&AW had been working tirelessly to gather enough evidence to bring him to justice and put an end to his reign of terror.

In addition to his direct involvement in terrorist activities, Malik Al-Hassan was also implicated in numerous other crimes, including money laundering, arms trafficking, and kidnapping. He had amassed a vast fortune through his illicit enterprises, using his wealth to fund further acts of violence and expand his criminal empire. Despite his efforts to evade capture, R&AW finally managed to gather enough evidence to secure his arrest. In a coordinated operation, they apprehended Malik Al-Hassan and his associates, dismantling his criminal network and putting an end to his reign of terror.

Malik Al-Hassan's arrest was a significant victory for R&AW and a triumph for justice. It sent a clear message to other would-be criminals that no one is above the law and that those who sow chaos and destruction will be held accountable for their actions.

***

A long time ago, Zoya, Rashid, and Malik Al Hassan were like three peas in a pod. They worked together in a secret team before the creation of Obsidian Dawn, going on daring and dangerous missions to make the world a safer place.

In their top-secret headquarters, they would gather around maps and plans, plotting their next move. "We need to act fast," Rashid would say, his voice urgent. "Our target won't wait around for us."s

Zoya would nod, her eyes serious. "Let's gather all the info we can before we make our move," she'd suggest, calm and collected.

Their adventures took them to faraway lands, from busy markets to empty deserts. No matter where they went, they stuck together like glue, supporting each other through thick and thin.

Sometimes, they'd find themselves in tight spots, but they always managed to escape.

"Remember that time in Cairo?" Zoya would laugh, remembering a narrow escape from some bad guys.

Malik would grin, the memory still fresh in his mind. "How could I forget? We barely made it out of there in one piece!" he'd say, chuckling along with her.

Even when they disagreed, they still had each other's backs. "We might not always agree, but we're a team," Rashid would remind them, his voice full of determination.

But as time went on, things started to change. Disagreements turned into arguments, and secrets began to drive them apart.

Despite their differences, they still tried to work together. "We need to stick to the plan," Zoya would insist, her voice firm.

Malik would shake his head, his patience wearing thin. "We need to rethink our strategy," he'd say, his tone serious.

But no matter how hard they tried, they couldn't seem to see eye-to-eye anymore. Betrayals and lies tore at the fabric of their friendship, leaving them divided and alone.

In the end, their once-unbreakable bond was shattered, leaving them on opposite sides of a bitter feud.

Zoya and Rashid's paths diverged from Malik's when they joined the Obsidian Dawn, driven by different motives and ideals. While Zoya and Rashid saw the organization as a means to achieve their goals and make a difference in the world, Malik was driven solely by his own ambitions and desires for power. From the moment they joined the Obsidian Dawn, it became clear that

Malik's intentions were not aligned with theirs. He showed little regard for the organization's principles and values, viewing it merely as a stepping stone to further his own agenda. Zoya and Rashid, on the other hand, were committed to the cause, willing to sacrifice their own interests for what they believed was the greater good. They worked tirelessly to advance the Obsidian Dawn's goals, while Malik refused to take orders from anyone.

As tensions within the organization grew, fueled by Malik's selfish actions and disregard for the chain of command, Zoya and Rashid found themselves at odds with their former ally. It became increasingly clear that their paths were no longer aligned, and they ultimately made the difficult decision to part ways with Malik and forge their own destiny within the Obsidian Dawn.

Though their separation was fraught with conflict and uncertainty, Zoya and Rashid remained steadfast in their commitment to the cause they believed in.

However, Rashid and Zoya never forgot Malik. Rashid had demanded the release of Malik Al Hassan as a crucial component of a high-stakes deal with the head of R&AW; this demand stemmed from Rashid's strategic calculations and perhaps personal motivations.

Rashid viewed Malik as a valuable asset with significant influence or power. Releasing Malik was advantageous for Rashid's plans, whether it was to gain his support, leverage his resources, or neutralize potential threats. Rashid believed that by securing Malik's freedom, he could strengthen his own position within the complex web of alliances and rivalries. Rashid also had specific plans or agendas that required Malik's involvement; he saw Malik as a key player in a larger scheme or as someone whose skills and connections were essential for achieving certain objectives. By securing Malik's release, Rashid could have been positioning himself for future collaborations or partnerships that would advance his own interests or the goals of the Obsidian Dawn.

On a personal level, Rashid might have harbored loyalty or respect for Malik, viewing him as a trusted ally or friend. This motivated Rashid to negotiate for Malik's freedom.

***

The news of the failed deal with Malik Al Hassan sent shockwaves through the R&AW headquarters. Tony, Sikandar, and Yuvraj Singhania wasted no time in convening an emergency meeting to assess the situation and chart a course of action.

Tony's brow furrowed in concern as he addressed the gathered officials. "This turn of events changes everything. We need to reassess our approach and prepare for the repercussions."

Sikandar nodded in agreement, his expression grim. "We must anticipate Malik's next move. He has connections and won't take this setback lightly, and we need to be ready for any retaliatory actions."

Yuvraj Singhania, his voice measured, added, "We must also consider the implications of our agents and defense dignitaries being captured. We must prioritize their safety and devise a plan to secure their release."

As they deliberated on their next steps, the gravity of the situation weighed heavily on everyone present. The stakes were higher than ever, and failure was not an option.

"We need to act swiftly and decisively," Tony asserted, his tone resolute. "Every minute counts, and we can't afford to hesitate."

Sikandar leaned forward, his gaze intense. "We must mobilize all available resources and launch a comprehensive operation to contain the fallout from this failed deal."

Yuvraj Singhania nodded in agreement, his expression somber. "Our priority must be to safeguard national security and protect our agents and dignitaries at all costs."

"Keep a close eye on those three," Yuvraj said. "All of them are criminal masterminds – make sure they don't cook up something behind our backs."

Tony, Sikandar, and Yuvraj Singhania continued to strategize and coordinate their response to the unfolding crisis. With determination and resolve, they vowed to navigate the challenges ahead and emerge victorious in their mission to protect the country and its citizens.

As the meeting drew to a close, the R&AW officials dispersed, each tasked with specific responsibilities to address the crisis at hand. The coming days will test their resolve and determination like never before.

In the cramped confines of their cell, Tony and Sikandar watched over Zoya, Rashid, and Malik, their eyes narrowed with suspicion as they monitored their every move. "Keep an eye on them," Tony ordered, his voice low and menacing. "We can't afford to let them out of our sight for a second."

But despite the close scrutiny, Zoya, Rashid, and Malik exchanged furtive glances, their minds racing with plans and strategies. "We need to find a way to communicate without them knowing," Zoya whispered, her voice barely above a whisper.

Rashid nodded in agreement, his eyes darting around the room for any potential means of covert communication. "We'll have to be clever about it," he replied, his voice tinged with determination.

As they bided their time, Tony and Sikandar remained vigilant, their presence a constant reminder of the danger that lurked around every corner. But the three prisoners refused to be intimidated, their resolve unshaken despite the odds stacked against them.

Without warning, Tony and Sikandar barged into the interrogation room, staring menacingly at Rashid. Zoya watched helplessly from a corner, her heart pounding with fear and anger; while Malik was watching, his jaw dropped.

"You thought you could outsmart us, huh?" Tony sneered, his voice dripping with malice as he raised a clenched fist.

Rashid met Tony's gaze with steely determination, refusing to show any sign of weakness. "I won't beg for mercy from the likes of you," he retorted defiantly.

Without a word, Tony swung his fist, the blow landing squarely on Rashid's jaw with a sickening thud. Rashid's head snapped to the side, pain shooting through his body, but he gritted his teeth and refused to cry out. "You three are going to regret crossing us," Sikandar growled, his voice low and menacing as he stepped forward, his knuckles cracking ominously.

Rashid braced himself for the next blow, steeling himself against the pain as he prepared to endure whatever punishment they meted out. "I won't break," he vowed, his voice barely a whisper but filled with unwavering resolve.

With a cruel laugh, Tony delivered another brutal blow, the force of it causing Rashid's vision to swim. But still, he remained steadfast, his spirit unbroken despite the agony coursing through his body. As the beatings continued, Zoya's heart ached with helplessness and rage. "You're not going to break us." Tony and Sikandar, however, smiled and continued their assault, intent on making an example of Rashid to assert their dominance and quash any hope of resistance.

Through the haze of pain, Rashid clung to a flicker of defiance, refusing to give his tormentors the satisfaction of seeing him falter. "We'll never give up," he vowed.

"Good luck with that," Tony scoffed as he and Sikandar left the room. Despite facing physical intimidation from Tony and Sikandar, Zoya, Rashid, and Malik refused to cower in fear. The blows landed on Rashid by their captors only fueled their determination to resist. In the dimly lit cell, the three captives sat in silence, contemplating their next move. Despite the obstacles and the watchful eyes of Tony and Sikandar, they knew that giving up was not an option. Their resolve to survive and resist grew stronger, even in the face of overwhelming odds.

Chapter 15

Shadows and Light

The hum of equipment filled a bleak and cramped room as Tony and Sikandar oversaw the enhancement of their monitoring system. Now that Zoya, Rashid, and Malik were held captive, they needed to bolster all existing operations.

Banks of panels showed various camera feeds, and the odd beep or buzz indicated that an additional layer of security had been installed. It was a necessary measure, as instructed by the Head of R&AW, Yuvraj Singhania, who was given regular updates about the captives.

"Make sure every corner is covered," Tony ordered, adjusting a new camera's angle. "I want no blind spots."

Sikandar nodded, typing swiftly on his keyboard.

"This new software should make it nearly impossible for them to communicate without us knowing. They won't stand a chance."

Across the corridor in their makeshift jail cell, Rashid and Zoya exchanged worried glances. They could hear the sounds of drills and footsteps, signaling the tightening of security measures.

"You hear that? We need to find a way to communicate," Zoya whispered, her voice barely audible. "If they catch us planning, we're done for."

"We have to be smart about this. They're watching our every move," Rashid replied with a nod, his eyes scanning the room for any potential way to bypass the new system.

In a separate corner of the room, Malik sat unfazed. Unbeknownst to Zoya, Rashid, and the agents of R&AW, he had been hatching something.

As if on cue, the door creaked open, revealing Tony's stern face.

"Time for a change of scenery," he sneered, signaling for two guards to enter.

Rashid, Zoya, and Malik were quickly separated, each escorted down a maze-like corridor to a different cell. The cold, sterile walls seemed to close in on them, amplifying their feelings of isolation.

In his new cell, Rashid paced restlessly. The air was laden with inexplicable tension, the weight of the situation pressing down on him.

Meanwhile, Zoya found herself in a similar predicament. Alone in her cell, she sat on the cold floor, her mind racing with thoughts of survival.

Malik remained in the room, bound and equally helpless, or so the others thought.

Back in the monitoring room, Sikandar smirked as he watched the screens.

"Separating the three was a good call," he remarked. "They won't be able to conspire now."

"Let's see them try to outsmart us now," Tony said, reentering the room with a wide grin on his face. Unknown to Tony and Sikandar, Rashid, Zoya, and Malik were already concocting a plan. Separated but not defeated, they communicated ingeniously through a series of coded messages, using anything they could find – tapping on pipes, Morse code blinks, and even whispers that carried through the ventilation system.

Even though the odds were fully stacked against them, Rashid and Zoya weren't the type to give up without a fight.

Meanwhile, Tony and Sikandar sat in front of the bank of screens, their fingers dancing over the keyboard, switching between camera feeds. Their plan had evolved;

it was no longer merely about physical barriers but psychological warfare.

"I think we need to employ a few classic tactics on our prisoners," Tony smirked, pondering over a feed that showed Rashid pacing in his cell. "Let's see how they handle a little… *isolation*."

Sikandar nodded, his eyes scanning the monitors.

"For Zoya, let's try a different approach," he said, switching to Zoya's feed, showing her sitting alone, lost in thought. "Loneliness can be a powerful weapon."

As it happened, Malik was not exempt from these psychological games either. They had hacked into his communications, sending him misleading messages, making him feel threatened and suspicious to throw him off guard.

Feeling the weight of his isolation, Rashid shouted towards the ceiling, "You think this will break me? I've faced worse than this!"

"Oh, Rashid, this is just the beginning. How long do you think you can last without your precious Zoya by your side?" Tony chuckled, hearing Rashid's outburst. "And Malik… we all know he only looks out for himself."

Hearing Tony's taunts, Zoya clenched her fists, determined not to let them see her falter.

"I don't need Rashid to survive," she whispered to herself, trying to drown out the lingering doubts.

Soon, Sikandar decided he would be the one to 'break' Malik, a task that proved harder than he anticipated.

"Rashid and Zoya are weak. They'll betray you, you do know that?"

Although Malik was all too familiar with these tactics, Sikandar's words struck a chord, making him second-guess his alliance with them.

"You can save your breath," he spat, rolling his eyes.

"You guys have quite the history. But I guess loyalties change…" Sikandar remarked, pacing in circles around him.

Malik looked up at him, squinting his eyes.

"I don't care about loyalty. Everyone only does what serves their own interest."

"You better watch your back. A man alone in the world… is a dangerous thing," Sikandar scoffed, kneeling down.

Malik turned his head away, his jaw tight and his lips quivering. Sikandar left the room after delivering the blow, smiling at his handiwork. Later, he met up with Tony in the surveillance room, the sense of victory dripping from his face.

"Perfect. He's starting to doubt them," he muttered to himself with a smirk, remembering Malik's reaction.

Back in their cells, Rashid and Zoya couldn't help but feel trapped. The constant surveillance, the mind games, and the doubts were all taking their toll on them.

"I know what they're trying to do," Rashid whispered, trying to keep his voice steady. "We can't let them get to us."

"We have to stick it out. For ourselves and for each other," Zoya nodded, her eyes shining with resolve.

Little did Tony and Sikandar realize that their games were having the opposite effect on their captives. Instead of breaking their morale, it was strengthening their determination. Rashid and Zoya continued to communicate in coded whispers, reassuring each other and plotting their next move in the shadows, with Malik having a plan of his own.

"We'll show them," Rashid muttered, his voice laden with renewed purpose. "We'll show them that their games won't work on us."

As the hours passed, Tony and Sikandar grew frustrated, a stark contrast from their initial sense of triumph. Their psychological tactics were failing, and Rashid, Zoya, and Malik were proving to be more resilient than they had estimated. The battle of wills had begun, and Tony and Sikandar were about to learn that Rashid, Zoya, and Malik were not easily broken. Rashid and Zoya had plotted their escape - it was an elaborate plan that they would have to execute with the utmost precision. They had managed to pry open a small vent in the corner of their room, hoping it would lead to an access tunnel. Their objective was simple: gather resources, make their way through the tunnel, rescue Malik, and find a way out of the facility. Muddling over the details, Rashid and Zoya sat in silence, each lost in their thoughts. They had come so close, yet the reality of their situation couldn't be clearer: escaping would be far more difficult than they had imagined.

But despite the setback, their spark of determination remained. Now that they had come this far, they weren't about to give up at any cost. They would learn from their mistakes, adapt their plans, and continue to fight for their freedom.

Amid her plotting, Zoya found a folded piece of paper in her cell slipped through the crevice under the door. She wondered where it had come from, seeing as she had not heard or seen anyone outside. Unfolding it carefully, she found a cryptic message written in hurried handwriting:

'The key to freedom lies where the shadows meet the light.'

Zoya's eyes widened, hope shining in them.

"Is this… a clue? Is help on the way?" she asked herself, studying the message intently.

Cradling the note in her hands, she frowned, her instincts warning her to be cautious.

"It could be," she replied slowly, "or it could be a trap."

Yet, despite her reservations, curiosity got the better of her. That night, under the cover of darkness, Zoya followed the instructions from the cryptic message. She looked around her cell, searching for a place where the shadow indeed met the light - cast by a solitary overhead lamp. Then, she discovered a loose floor tile in the corner of her cell. "This must be it," she whispered, her heart racing. Her hands trembled as she lifted the tile, revealing a small compartment underneath. Inside, she found a set of keys and a note that read:

'Use these to unlock your path to freedom. Meet me behind the crimson door.'

Little did she know, it was all a setup - courtesy of R&AW and their ability to always remain one step ahead.

Sure enough, Zoya's excitement was short-lived. As soon as she picked up the key, she pried it in the cell door. To her immense shock, it flung open almost instantly.

With a sigh of relief, Zoya followed the instructions scribbled on the note to find a crimson door. After sneaking and tiptoeing throughout the facility, Zoya felt an air of suspicion creeping up in her spine. Her heart hammered a frantic rhythm against her ribs as she crept down the sterile corridor, the fluorescent lights flickering above. In the strained calm, the creak of her sneakers on the smooth floor sounded like a gunshot.

With each twitch of her tense fingers, the note she held in her moist palm crinkled. It was the only thing keeping her alive—a mysterious note from an unknown person that promised freedom. Reaching for a dented metal door with peeling and chipped scarlet paint, she prayed silently. If the note was to be believed, this was her way out.

Suddenly, Zoya's breath hitched in her throat. Behind that door could be freedom or something far worse. Steeling her nerves, she reached for the handle, the cold metal sending a jolt through her. A couple of twists of the key and her fate would be sealed – either way. She finally opened the door to see Rashid sitting there, desolated and bound. He looked up, alarmed to see her.

"Zoya?" he gasped, his mouth open and eyes wide.

"Rashid?" Zoya said, peering at him.

And then, it hit her: this was a trap.

All of a sudden, alarms started blaring throughout the facility, lights flashing brightly. Before they could think or react, the lights in the chamber stopped flickering.

"Well, well, what do we have here? You sure fell for it," a voice echoed, revealing Tony and Sikandar, who emerged from the shadows.

Zoya's heart sank, realization dawning on her.

"You… slipped the note under my door," she rasped, disbelief evident in her eyes.

"Did you really think we'd make it that easy for you?" Tony smirked.

"You underestimate us," Sikandar said with a laugh.

Rashid clenched the keys in his fist, anger bubbling up inside him.

"You won't break us," he spat out defiantly.

Zoya nodded, standing tall beside Rashid.

Tony simply shook his head.

***

In the aftermath of Zoya, Rashid, and Malik's failed attempt to escape and subsequent recapture, Yuvraj Singhania called for a meeting, his usually composed demeanor showing signs of irritation.

"Where do we stand?" he asked, his voice calm but with an edge of frustration. "How is it possible that we have not been able to get even one of them talking as yet?"

Tony and Sikandar exchanged nervous glances, beads of sweat forming on their brows. They knew they were in deep trouble.

"Sir, we have been trying our best," Tony admitted, his voice barely audible over the hum of the monitors. "But at least they are in our cust-"

Yuvraj's eyes narrowed slightly. "In our custody? You fools! Those three operatives are some of the most dangerous on our watchlist! Merely imprisoning them isn't enough!"

Tony shifted uncomfortably under Yuvraj's gaze. "We'll do whatever it takes to rectify this situation, sir. We promise."

But Yuvraj was not appeased. "Promises? I want action, not words. And I want it now."

As Tony and Sikandar scrambled to devise a plan, the atmosphere in the control room grew tense. Every passing second felt like an eternity, the weight of their failure pressing down on them.

Finally, Tony spoke up, his voice trembling with uncertainty. "Sir, maybe we should interrogate one of them… more harshly. That would send a message to the others."

Yuvraj nodded, "Yes, extract the information we need by any means possible. Pick one of them and get it done."

Tony and Sikandar exchanged hesitant glances, the weight of their decision heavy on their shoulders. Rashid, Zoya, and Malik had been their captives for weeks now, but they still knew little about them or their intentions.

Yuvraj's patience was wearing thin, "Well, gentlemen?

"We'll… get right on it, sir," Tony responded.

"Good. Now get out," Yuvraj gestured towards the door.

They left Yuvraj's office, the pressure building, as they prepared to take action.

"I say we start with Rashid," Tony suggested, his voice wavering slightly. "He's the more vocal of the two. Maybe he'll crack under pressure."

Sikandar hesitated. "But Zoya... she's no pushover either. And she's got connections. Maybe she knows something we don't. As far as Malik goes, I have a feeling he won't say much. He's going to be a tough nut to crack; man's practically been through hell."

Sikandar ran a hand through his hair, his brow furrowed in deep concentration. "We can't afford to make the wrong decision," he muttered.

Tony nodded in agreement, his mind racing with conflicting thoughts. “Let’s take out Malik. Who knows what secrets she’s hiding? Rashid might crack under pressure, but Zoya... she’s a wildcard.”

“We need to think this through carefully,” Sikandar said. “We can’t rush into this blindly.”

Tony nodded, his jaw set in determination. “Agreed.”

As they contemplated the decision, they realized they were at a stalemate: there was only one option left, as suggested by Tony.

“Want to flip a coin?” he said in a manner that, on the surface, seemed humorous.

“Really?” Sikandar sneered.

“Do you have any other bright ideas?”

“Well… no. Fine, a coin it is. Heads for Rashid, Tails for Zoya,” Sikandar pulled a nickel out of his pants.

As the coin spun through the air, landing with a metallic clink on the cold concrete floor, Tony and Sikandar shared an apprehensive glance.

“Are you ready for this?” Tony asked Sikandar, his expression grim.

"I am if you are."

Without wasting a moment, Tony and Sikandar approached the prison cell; their footsteps echoed ominously in the dimly lit corridor. The heavy metal door loomed before them, a barrier between them and the truth they sought.

With a silent exchange of nods, they steeled themselves and pushed open the door, the hinges groaning in protest. The sight that greeted them inside sent a chill down their spines. Zoya sat on the narrow cot, her back rigid with tension as she met their gaze with unyielding defiance. The air crackled with strain as they entered, the weight of their intentions hanging heavy in the air. Tony cleared his throat. "*Zoya*. We need to… talk."

Zoya's eyes narrowed, her lips pressed into a thin line. "I'm listening."

Sikandar took a steady step forward. "We know you're hiding something, Zoya. And we're not leaving until you tell us what it is."

Zoya's jaw tightened, but she refused to back down. "I don't know what you're talking about."

Tony exchanged a knowing look with Sikandar, their silent communication speaking volumes. They were determined to get to the bottom of this, no matter what it took. With a shared sense of resolve, Tony and Sikandar pressed Zoya for answers, their interrogation relentless and unforgiving. But as the hours dragged on, it became increasingly clear that Zoya would not crack easily.

The tension in the room reached a boiling point as accusations flew and tempers flared. But amidst the chaos, one thing remained certain: Tony and Sikandar were not leaving until they got the answers they sought.

They started with the basics: verbal threats and intimidation. Tony's voice dripped with malice as he leaned in close, his breath hot against Zoya's ear. "You think you can outsmart us, Zoya? You think you can keep your secrets hidden forever?"

Zoya gritted her teeth, refusing to give them the satisfaction of seeing her flinch. "I won't... tell you anything." With Zoya unrelenting, the interrogation stretched into the night, the fate of everyone involved hung in the balance, the truth lurking just out of reach. In an effort to extract as much information from her as soon as possible since Yuvraj was breathing down their necks, they had to resort to more brutal methods of fishing for the truth.

Zoya found herself subjected to a barrage of relentless torture methods, each more cruel than the last. Tony and Sikandar were determined to break her resolve, to force her to reveal the truth behind their final plan.

It didn't take long before they moved on to physical torture, their methods designed to inflict maximum pain while leaving minimal evidence. They strapped Zoya to a metal chair, her wrists and ankles bound tight with unforgiving restraints.

Sikandar brandished a length of electrical wire, his eyes glinting with sadistic pleasure. "Let's see how long you can keep silent under a little pressure, Zoya."

With a flick of his wrist, Sikandar sent a surge of electricity coursing through Zoya's body, her muscles seizing up as she screamed out in pain. But still, she refused to break, her willpower stronger than any physical torment they could inflict.

Frustrated, Tony and Sikandar escalated their tactics, resorting to psychological torture to wear down Zoya's defenses. They played mind games, planting seeds of doubt and fear in her mind, hoping to erode her resolve from the inside out.

"You're alone, Zoya," Tony taunted, his tone like ice. "No one is coming to save you. You might as well give up now and save yourself the trouble."

But Zoya remained defiant, her spirit unbroken despite the relentless onslaught. She knew she couldn't give in, not when so much was at stake. She bit back the pain, refusing to let them see her weakness. But she could only take so much before her body broke down.

Zoya clenched her jaw, her mind racing as she weighed her options and winced in pain. She knew she had to buy time, to delay revealing their plans for as long as possible. But with every passing moment, the pressure mounted, and she felt herself nearing her breaking point.

"I swear I don't know what you're talking about," Zoya shot back defiantly.

But Tony and Sikandar weren't convinced. They pressed on, their tactics growing more aggressive as they sought to wear down Zoya's defenses.

"We know about the deal Rashid made," Sikandar interjected, his tone laced with menace. "The weapons, the technology—you and Rashid were planning something big, weren't you?"

Zoya's heart pounded in her chest as she struggled to maintain her composure. She didn't want them to see her fear and let them break her resolve, but she eventually cracked.

Finally, with a heavy sigh, she revealed the details of their plan. She spoke of the weapons, the technology, and the elaborate scheme Rashid had concocted to ensure their success.

"They... they wanted the best weapons... the latest technology," Zoya spoke in a voice barely above a whisper. Her eyes darted nervously around the room, fear evident in every glance. Tony leaned forward. "What kind of weapons? What are you all planning?"

Zoya swallowed hard before continuing, "We... wanted... wanted to cause chaos, to disrupt... to make a statement," She struggled to find the right words.

Sikandar's brow furrowed in confusion. "A statement?"

"We wanted to show the world... show them what we were capable of… and to strike fear into the hearts of our enemies."

"And what about you, Zoya?" Tony asked. "What was your role in all of this?"

Zoya lowered her gaze, her hands trembling in her lap. "I... I was supposed to be the distraction," she admitted, her voice barely audible. "I was supposed to draw your attention away from the real plan."

Tony and Sikander had gotten what they wanted, and they had something substantial to report to Yuvraj. Still, as they left the room after hearing what they needed to do, the gravity of the situation sunk in.

***

As the sun set and darkness settled over the city, the R&AW team gathered at Yuvraj Singhania's house for a meeting. They sat around the dining table, glasses clinking and conversation buzzing.

"So, what's the final word on the case?" Yuvraj asked, looking around at his team.

"Well, it's been a rollercoaster ride, but we've made some progress," Tony replied, sipping his drink.

"Yeah, we've had our ups and downs, but I think we're finally getting somewhere. Tihar will do a number on them," Sikandar chimed in.

Yuvraj nodded, listening intently to their reports. "I'm proud of all the hard work you've put in. It hasn't been easy, but we're getting closer to cracking this case."

As they discussed the details of their investigation, laughter filled the room, and the mood lightened. They toasted on their teamwork and determination, celebrating their successes and sharing stories from the field.

As the evening wore on, Yuvraj raised his glass for a final toast. "To a job well done and a case closed," he said, smiling at his team.

Tony, Sikandar, and the others echoed his sentiment, clinking their glasses together before bidding each other goodnight. As they left, there was a sense of accomplishment in the air, a feeling that they had overcome the odds and emerged victorious once again.

They thought the case was finally closed and they could move on to the next assignment.

Little did they know, however, that their journey had only just begun. Unknown to them, new challenges lurked in the shadows, waiting to test their skills and resolve once again. Despite the apparent victory, the night held an air of uncertainty, hinting at the trials yet to come. In their cells, Rashid, Zoya, and Malik remained resolute. They knew their fight was far from over. With unwavering determination, they vowed to find a way to expose the truth and reclaim their freedom, no matter the cost.

The battle lines were drawn, and the game of cat and mouse continued, but one thing was certain: Rashid, Zoya, and Malik were not defeated. They were merely biding their time, waiting for the right moment to strike back.

And as the dawn broke, a new day began – one filled with hope, defiance, and the relentless pursuit of justice. The end was not written yet, and the story of Rashid, Zoya, and Malik would continue would continue as long as they were alive, their spirits unbroken and their will unyielding.

www.ingramcontent.com/pod-product-compliance
Lightning Source LLC
LaVergne TN
LVHW091319150826
845673LV00006B/1699

* 9 7 9 8 8 9 5 4 4 5 9 9 0 *